THE
DRUID
— AND THE —
DRAGON

KRISTIN BUTCHER

CP | CRWTH PRESS

Library and Archives Canada Cataloguing in Publication

Title: The druid and the dragon / Kristin Butcher.
Names: Butcher, Kristin, 1951- author.
Identifiers: Canadiana (print) 20200264508 | Canadiana
(ebook) 20200264532 | ISBN 9781989724033
(softcover) | ISBN 9781989724040 (EPUB)

Classification: LCC PS8553.U6972 D78 2020 | DDC jC813/.54—dc23

Cover illustration by Rubén Carral Fajardo
Cover and interior design by Julia Breese
Copy edited by Laura Langston
Proofread by Audrey McClellan

Published by
Crwth Press
#204 – 2320 Woodland Drive
Vancouver, BC V5N 3P2
778-302-5525

Printed and bound in Canada.

23 22 21 20 · 4 3 2 1

DEDICATION

For Elle, who helped me understand it
would take a trilogy to tell Maeve's story.

DRUID and the DRAGON MAP

NORTHERN SEA

EASTERN PASS

WESTERN PASS

KING'S CASTLE

NORTH COUNTRY

NEWGRANGE

MEATH

CASTLE CARRICK

DRUID CAMP

DRAGON CAVE

VILLAGE

EASTERN SEA

CHAPTER 1

Maeve gasped as the knobby end of her mother's broom dug into her back.

"Wake up, daughter. Can you not keep your mind on your work for even a minute? Those pans won't wash themselves."

"The water's cold," Maeve mumbled. "And it's greasy."

"I shouldn't wonder," her mother said. "You have cleaned but one pan this whole morning." She scowled and wagged her broom toward the open door of the cottage. "You need to start over. There's a pot of water on the fire in the yard." When Maeve didn't move, she added, "What are you waiting for? Fetch it. And this time make good use of it." She clucked her tongue. "Some days I swear your head is filled with straw."

Maeve wiped her wet hands on her apron and gripped the sides of the wash pan tightly before easing it off the table and lumbering across the cottage to the door.

"Don't be slopping dirty water," her mother called after her. "I'll not thank you for a mud floor."

Though Maeve moved carefully, the murky water lapped the sides of the pan, climbing closer to the rim with every step. She managed to get outside without spilling, only to trip over her own feet once past the doorsill. As she tried to regain her balance, she lost her hold on the pan and down it went.

"Don't dump it here!" her sister, Deirdre, wailed as the water splatted the hard earth and jumped back up to splash the wooden vat where she was scrubbing clothes.

Maeve chased after the runaway pan. "Sorry." The word rushed from her lips without her even thinking it. She was always in trouble for something, so apologies came as naturally as breathing.

Maeve supposed she deserved most of the tongue-lashings that came her way. Her mind did wander. She was often distracted, even when she was trying her hardest not to be. She had no control over the curious things that wandered in and out of her head. Some were so strange not even she understood what they meant or why she thought them.

This morning was a perfect example. She'd been concentrating on washing the pots when a breeze had blown in through the window—and then into her head—sweeping her thoughts away as thoroughly as her mother's broom swept the floor. Taking their place was a vision so bizarre, Maeve had no notion what to make of it. A rush of images spun through her head—castles and kings, snow, fierce warriors, crows and even a dragon, all pulsing in and out of focus. Why would she think of such things?

Maeve knew of no one else whose mind played

strange tricks—certainly not her parents or sister. She seldom told anyone her visions. Most of the villagers already believed she was a simpleton. If they knew about her bizarre imaginings, they'd think she was mad as a rabid dog.

Perhaps she was. Though she hated to think it, she knew she was different. It was a lonely reality.

For the remainder of the morning Maeve did her best to keep her mind on her chores. She couldn't allow herself to be distracted by a single thing. She didn't want to give her mother any excuse to keep her working through the afternoon. Not today.

It was Maeve's turn to sell eggs in the village, and she was very much looking forward to it. It was a break from the endless stream of chores at the cottage. It was also a chance to be among people—even if most only paid her heed because of the eggs. That didn't stop her from watching and listening. She could almost pretend she was one of them.

The best part of afternoons spent in the village, though, was Declan. He always seemed to show up on the days she was there. Perhaps he came every day. Maeve didn't know. For her, it was enough that he was there when she was. Whenever she was with him, she felt as light as dandelion fluff. He was the only person she dared share her thoughts with.

———

Maeve left for the village after the midday meal. She was so anxious to be away, it was all she could do to keep from running straight for the woods. She felt like a different person when she was in the forest, and today was no exception. The instant she stepped among the trees, her troubles fell at her feet like autumn leaves. She ambled aimlessly, staring up into the treetops, her thoughts flying on the wind. She chased after squirrels and gathered wildflowers. It was wonderful. No one chastised her for daydreaming. No one reminded her there was work to be done. No one made her feel small and stupid.

Of course, she reached the village later than she should have, so forcing her happy thoughts and feelings to the back of her mind, she set to work hawking her eggs. Her version of hawking, at any rate. While other peddlers shouted the merits of their wares and waved them in the air, pressing passersby to take a closer look, Maeve walked quietly up and down the road, presenting herself timidly to villagers.

"Fresh eggs today, mistress?" she said quietly to a woman who was trying to hang on to her shopping basket while herding three small children.

The woman frowned and made a grab for a little girl about to escape. "What's 'at? Speak up, girl."

"Would you like some eggs?" Maeve repeated, quiet as ever.

"If you're givin' 'em away, o' course I would," the woman snorted.

Maeve shook her head and lowered her eyes. "Sorry to trouble you."

As she started to turn away, the woman heaved a sigh. "Hang on. They're fresh, you say?"

Maeve brightened. "Yes. I collected them myself this morning."

The woman thrust the arm of the little girl at Maeve. "All right, then. I'll take three. Hang on to this little beggar while I find me pennies."

And so it went. As Maeve wandered up and down the street, her basket became lighter. The villagers picked through it, looking for eggs that suited them and then absently passing Maeve their coins without so much as a *please* or *thank you* or *good afternoon to you*. Maeve might as well have been invisible. But it was still preferable to being berated by her mother.

Maeve had never understood why her mother was so unpleasant, especially toward her. It was as if she disliked her. But how was that possible? Mothers didn't dislike their children. Maeve looked around at the mothers and children on the street. There were babes in arms, toddlers hanging on to their mothers' skirts, and boys and girls of all ages running everywhere, squealing and playing tag among the shoppers. Mothers shook fingers and pulled ears, but they also pushed back hair, pinched cheeks and smiled. Maeve couldn't remember her mother smiling at her even once. She'd had her cheek pinched often enough, but only in a way that left a bruise.

5

She frowned. It was different with Deirdre. Oh, her sister didn't receive any smiles either—Bronagh, wife of Eamon, didn't smile at anyone. And Deirdre also knew the sharp end of their mother's tongue. Still, there was something between the two, a bond Maeve wasn't privy to. She thought of her mother and sister working side by side in the field and over the cooking fire, carrying water together or changing the straw on the pallets. They seldom spoke, but the silence they shared seemed amiable. How Maeve wished she had that.

Had she and her mother always been distant? She tried to imagine herself as a baby, tried to make her mother smile down at her. But the face of the woman in her mind was as cold and hard as ever it had been.

And then—as if a wave had washed through her head—Maeve's mother's face became Deirdre's face. As Deirdre gazed down at the child in her arms, she *did* smile—a smile so deep Maeve could see straight into her heart, and she couldn't help smiling herself. That was what a mother was supposed to be like.

"How many eggs are left in your basket?"

Startled from her thoughts, Maeve spun toward the voice.

Declan grinned at her. "What faraway land were you visiting just now?"

Maeve frowned. She was embarrassed to have been caught daydreaming again and blurted the first thing that popped into her head. "If you must know, I was thinking about you."

Declan pulled back in surprise. "Me?"

Maeve nodded. "Yes, I was thinking how pleasant it must be to be you."

Declan frowned. "What makes you think my life is more pleasant than yours?"

"You're a Druid," she replied with a shrug, implying no further explanation was needed. But even to her own ears, her words sounded like an accusation.

Though they were highly revered, Druids kept themselves separate. They were wise and learned. Druids were teachers and seers and bards. They settled disputes and gave guidance, but no one knew much about them. They were mysterious, but part of the elite of the land nevertheless. There were kings and chieftains, and after them the Druids. Then there was everyone else.

To her surprise, Declan threw back his head and laughed, causing the hood of his mantle to slide off and set free a wild mop of curly black hair. "You think Druids have an easy life?" he said, his dark eyes glittering.

"Are you saying you don't?" Maeve replied, stretching an arm to take in the bustling village street. "The rest of us work our hands to the bone from sunup to sundown. All you do is walk about telling stories."

Inwardly, Maeve cringed. Why was she being so contrary? This morning she could think of

7

nothing better than seeing Declan. And now that he had appeared, she was being surly. It was as if it was her mother speaking and not her.

Declan crossed his arms over his chest. "Is that so?"

Maeve lifted her chin and bobbed her head.

He repeated his earlier question. "How many eggs do you have left?"

Maeve glanced into her basket. "Nine."

"Perfect. I shall buy them." He paused. "On one condition."

"What?" Maeve was suddenly leery.

"You let me show you how easy my life is."

Once they were away from the village and into the woods, Maeve's sour mood evaporated. She became herself again, walking happily at Declan's side.

"Where are we going?" she asked after they'd been walking for some time.

Declan shrugged and smiled. "You'll see."

After several more minutes he stopped, so Maeve did too. She peered around. The forest ahead looked much the same as that which lay behind them. "Why have we stopped?"

He put a finger to his lips and whispered, "Listen."

Maeve strained to hear something beyond the rustle of leaves in the breeze and the twitter of birds. At first there was nothing, but soon she became aware of a quiet hum. It wasn't like the buzz of bees or the lingering thrum of a plucked crwth string, but more like a collection of variant sounds—high and low, heavy and soft, dull and sharp—that came together to form one sound. As Maeve listened, a vision formed in her mind. Suddenly she knew exactly what she was hearing.

"Where?" she said, trying to see through the trees.

Declan smiled. "Follow me."

CHAPTER 2

As Declan stepped off the path into the undergrowth, he caught hold of Maeve's hand, and her
heart immediately began pounding like a hammer
in her chest. Before today, her mother was the
only one who'd ever held her hand, and it had
not been a pleasant experience. Hard work had
roughened her mother's skin, and a hard disposi-
tion had given her a grip fierce enough to cripple.
Declan's hand couldn't be more different. His skin
was warm and smooth, his grasp firm yet gentle.
Maeve allowed herself a contented smile.

Then just as quickly, her smile faded. Declan
was holding her hand—but what of it? That didn't
mean he liked her. He was leading her through a
part of the forest she didn't know, so it only made
sense to take her hand.

She was so befuddled by the situation that
when Declan unexpectedly stopped, she walked
straight into the back of him.

"I'm sorry," she squeaked. "I wasn't paying
attention." *Again*, she added crossly to herself.

"It is no matter," he replied, letting go of her
hand and pushing apart the foliage. "Look."

Maeve peered through the opening he'd
created, though her mind had already told her
what she would see.

It was a meadow surrounded by oak, yew and alder trees as well as gorse and ferns so dense it was hard to imagine anything beyond them. Nature's way of providing privacy. Not that the Druids were private. They mingled freely with the villagers and farmers. But they didn't live among them. Maeve marvelled that she had never wondered where they lived. Truthfully, until she met Declan, she had never thought of Druids at all.

But now she was intrigued. Dressed in robes of various colours and hooded mantles, they went about their business in the meadow. A middle-aged woman stirred a pot suspended over a small fire, while another carrying a basket rooted through the grass, picking greens. At the far side of the clearing, someone was chopping wood, while someone else was stacking it. Two men strolled the perimeter of the meadow, heads bent in conversation. A white-haired fellow with a long beard sat on a rotting log, nodding appreciatively to a lad playing a flute. The hum Maeve had detected from a distance had grown into the sounds of people busy with life.

As far as she could tell, the difference between Druids and other folk was not the things they did so much as how they did them. There was no urgency about the Druids. Purpose, yes, but no hurry or worry. It was as if they weren't troubled by the same concerns as ordinary people.

The thing that surprised Maeve was how few Druids there were—only eight that she could see. And though they seemed to be living in the meadow, there was little sign of their habitation. The grass still grew wild, and there were no dirt yards like she was used to seeing. Remove the people, and the only sign that they'd been in the meadow would be the remains of the fire.

She turned to Declan. "This is where you live?"

He smiled. "For now. It changes with the seasons—and with the needs of those who depend on us."

"That sounds like a riddle. I suppose that is why you are a bard. You are clever with words."

Declan shook his head. "I'm not a bard yet. I still have many, many stories to learn and put to memory before I can call myself that. My apprenticeship has barely begun. I have been at it but four years."

"Four!" Maeve exclaimed. "And you're still not done? How many years does it take?"

"About twenty. Though it is for my master, Finn, to decide when I am ready."

Maeve's jaw dropped. "That's so long!"

He shrugged. "There are many stories, and I must learn not only how to tell them, but their meaning and why they are important. I must also learn how to tell my own stories so that when this time we live in is gone, the bards who come after will be able to share those stories too."

Maeve eyed him dubiously. "What needs to be remembered about this time? Should my great-great-grandchildren know how many eggs I sold in the village today?" She smiled to let Declan know she was jesting.

He smiled too and winked at her. "You never know," he said. "The world may be quite different years from now, and it might help people understand how a lass spent her afternoons." His expression became serious once more. "You think there is nothing important about this time and place because you are living in it, but there is much that should be remembered."

"Like what?" Maeve pressed him.

"Well, for a start—our kings. Who are they and what do they do?"

"They go to war," she said. "I can't count how many times my father has had to put down his hammer and hoe so he can lift his sword for his king."

"And those are the sorts of stories I need to pass on," Declan said. "But enough of that. There is someone I would like you to meet. Come."

He led Maeve through the trees and into the meadow. Then, waving to the other Druids, he headed for the white-haired man on the log. As they approached, the boy with the flute left.

"Ah, young Declan, I see you have returned. And you have brought a friend." The old man smiled at Maeve. His expression was so welcoming, his eyes so blue, his voice so soothing.

"Bradan, this is Maeve," Declan said. "She is the blacksmith's daughter. She sells eggs in the village."

Bradan nodded. "Welcome, Maeve."

Maeve bobbed her head and smiled shyly. "Hello."

"Bradan is a seer," Declan said. "His counsel is much sought after by chieftains and kings."

Bradan laughed—a warm, rich sound that drew Maeve in. "The lad is easily impressed." Then he turned to Declan and his expression sobered. "Master Finn has been asking after you."

Declan turned to Maeve. "I must see what he wants. But I will be quick. Then I shall walk you back to your part of the forest. Bradan will keep you company until I return."

As Maeve watched Declan cross the clearing, it occurred to her that she was alone in a strange place, and she suddenly felt anxious.

"He will be but a few minutes," Bradan said.

Maeve was embarrassed to think her discomfort showed.

"It's refreshing to see a new face," the old man went on. "We don't get many visitors."

"Your camp is not easy to find," Maeve replied.

"True enough," he chuckled. "But you found it."

"Not really. Declan brought me here."

The old man nodded. "Perhaps, but you would have made your way to this place sooner or later."

"Why do you say that?"

"Some things a body knows." He placed a wrinkled hand on his chest and tapped his brow with the other. "It's a matter of listening to your heart and your head."

Maeve rolled her eyes. "Unless you have a crazy head like mine. Only a fool would heed the things that go through my mind. It's all nonsense."

Bradan shrugged. "Confusing perhaps. But nonsense?" He shook his head. "I doubt that. Your thoughts merely want clarity."

She regarded him curiously. "What do you mean?"

"Maeve!" Declan was waving from halfway across the meadow.

She returned his wave and then turned back to Bradan. "I must go."

"Yes," he replied. "You don't want to worry your mother. But do come back, young Maeve. We will talk again."

And they did. Maeve returned to the Druid camp with Declan several times in the weeks that followed. On each visit she spoke with Bradan, though no two conversations were ever the same. She loved that. At home she never got to express her ideas—about anything. As far as Maeve's mother was concerned, talking kept a body from working. Bradan had no such concerns. He liked to discuss everything—the weather, what went on in the village, Maeve's activities, her likes and dislikes, and even her innermost thoughts. The last always made her a bit uncomfortable, since she wasn't anxious to share a part of herself she didn't fully understand, but Bradan never criticized her or made her feel small in any way. He simply listened. After their conversations she always felt more at peace, and sometimes she found she didn't feel different from other people at all.

She was getting to know the other Druids too, particularly Enda, the healer. Enda was about twice Maeve's age, but from the moment Declan introduced them, Maeve was drawn to her. The woman had a perpetual twinkle in her eye, an infectious laugh and a warmth that immediately put a person at ease. She was a Druid, but she could just as easily have been a seller of pies in the village. The fact that she also knew all there was to know about plants and how to use them only served to make Maeve admire her more.

"How do you know which herbs are which?" Maeve asked as she watched Enda sort through her heaping basket of plants one afternoon, tying them together in bunches with strings of braided grass. Maeve scratched her head. The bundles laid out on the table all looked the same to her.

Enda laughed. "Practice."

"But how do you remember what they all do?"

"I've been at this most of my life," Enda said. "After a while a body doesn't have to think about it anymore. You just know. Everyone is like that about something."

Maeve shook her head. "Not me."

Enda regarded her skeptically. "You don't think so?"

Maeve shook her head again. "I would never be able to remember all these herbs. Some days

I can't even remember where I've put my apron. I'd end up making tea out of a poisonous plant or making salve with herbs meant to help a body sleep."

Enda laughed again. "You might not remember all the plants, but in time you'd learn a few. But there are other things you know without thinking."

"What?" Maeve couldn't imagine she knew much about anything, never mind know it without thinking.

Enda cocked her head in thought. "Your family raises chickens, yes?"

Maeve nodded warily.

"And you sell the eggs in the village?"

"Yes."

"Well, I've always been curious how a person knows which eggs are for selling and which are growing baby chicks."

Maeve's apprehension melted into relief, and she laughed. "You really don't know?"

Enda shrugged. "I'm a healer. I know plants— not eggs. But obviously *you* know."

"You hold them up to a lighted candle," Maeve explained. "If the inside of the egg is clear, it's for eating. If it's cloudy and hard to see through, it's probably growing a chick."

"But how can you be sure?"

"After you've done it a few times, you just know," said Maeve.

"I see," Enda said. "Much like a body might know which herbs do what, don't you think?" Her eyes were dancing, and the corners of her mouth were twitching.

Maeve sighed and rolled her eyes. "I suppose," she conceded, and they both laughed.

"Maeve!"

She looked across the meadow and saw Declan waving.

"Come on," he beckoned her. "It's time you got back."

Maeve said her good-byes to Enda, waved farewell to the other Druids and hurried after Declan, even though she didn't want to go. Home was a place that beat her down and broke her spirit. Here it was different. Maeve didn't understand the Druid beliefs or their ways, but they were kind and friendly. Visiting with them—even for an hour or two—always left her feeling better about herself.

Once she'd caught up to Declan, he turned his eyes to the sky, threw his arms wide and breathed deeply.

"'Has there ever been a more perfect day? Has the sky ever been bluer? Have the birds ever sung with fuller hearts?" He turned to Maeve. "Has the breeze ever caressed your skin so gently?"

Maeve lowered her gaze self-consciously. She was flustered and didn't know what to say. Clearly Declan had no such problem. There was no denying he knew how to weave words together. No wonder he'd been chosen to be the bard's apprentice.

He took hold of her hand. "Come," he grinned. "Let us not have this day spoiled by a scolding from your mother for being late. I'll race you to the rotting stump at the edge of your part of the forest!"

———

As she lay in bed that night, Maeve relived her afternoon at the Druid camp over and over in her mind. Declan was right. It *had* been a perfect day. She didn't want to fall asleep for then it would end, and in the morning she would once again be the blacksmith's strange daughter whose head was filled with nonsense.

Chapter 3

A few nights later, Maeve stopped climbing into the narrow bed she shared with her sister and gaped at Deirdre. "You're getting married?"

"Isn't that what I just said?" When Maeve still didn't move, Deirdre added, "Well, don't stand there like a fence post waiting for a pigeon. Get into bed."

When she did, Deirdre dragged the rough woolen blanket over them.

"Why didn't I know about this?" demanded Maeve in a hushed voice.

"Well, you aren't the one getting married, are you?" Deirdre whispered back.

"But Ma and Da haven't said a word."

"Not to you. Why would they?"

"I don't even know who you're marrying."

"Fergus, son of Conn." Deirdre lowered her voice even more. "From the moors on the other side of the village. Conn was a soldier in the Great King's army, but he lost an arm and gained a limp. Now he's a farmer, though it's mostly Fergus who works the land. But there's talk of war, and since Fergus is of an age, he'll probably join the fight."

"Who'll run the farm while he's gone?"

"His father isn't much use, so it would be up to his mother and younger brothers." There was

20

a short pause, and then she added, "And me, I suppose."

Their mother's voice cut through the night. "Stop your jabbering and get to sleep, the pair of you."

Maeve stared into the darkness. She couldn't believe her sister was getting married. It wasn't a situation *she* would want to be jumping into, but Deirdre seemed fine with it. She might not be giddy with excitement, but she didn't appear to be bothered either. It was rather like how a body handled the weather. You could wake up to sunshine or you could wake up to rain. Either way, you had to get on with your day.

"Do you even know him?" Maeve whispered in Deirdre's direction.

"I've seen him."

"Do you *want* to marry him?"

"What does that have to do with anything?" Deirdre growled and rolled away with the blanket.

Maeve grabbed hold of a corner and rolled the other way. "You don't have to, you know," she muttered into the warm air under the cover. "You can't be forced to marry. It's the law."

Deirdre flipped over and muttered crossly into Maeve's back. "Why would I object? I can't live with Ma and Da forever. If I marry Fergus, I will have a roof over my head and food on the table. My children will be cared for."

Maeve didn't want her sister to marry and leave. She would miss her. It was as simple as that. She hoped Deirdre might miss her a little too, but her sister was every bit as practical as their mother and likely wouldn't allow herself to think such a thing.

Maeve flipped over too, so that the sisters were nose to nose. "But you don't even know him!"

"So?" Deirdre hissed back. "If I'm sharing the man's house and bed, I imagine I'll get to know him well enough, soon enough. Sister, you have the strangest ideas about things. You'd best get your head around the notion of marriage, because it will soon be your turn."

———

Fergus and his family showed up in the yard three days later. Maeve's father gave Conn two chickens, and Conn offered up a pig in return. Then the marriage was finalized with a meal and several cups of mead. Maeve watched as if through a haze. The sets of parents sat across the table from each other, talking about the weather, the land and whatever else they could think of to fill the uncomfortable silences. It was clear they would all be relieved to go their separate ways.

As Maeve glanced around the small cottage, it struck her that everyone had brown hair and brown eyes. Not only Fergus's family, but both her parents and Deirdre too. She wound a curl of her own copper hair around her finger. As if the crazy thoughts that filled her head weren't enough to set her apart from everyone else, she had to look different too. Was that why her mother disliked her so?

When the meal was finally done, Deirdre left with her new husband and family without a backward glance. Maeve waved her on her way just the same.

That night Maeve had the narrow bed to herself. It felt strange—and empty. She and Deirdre had shared the same bed their entire lives. They knew each other better than either of them knew anyone else, and though they didn't always get along, there was an understanding between them.

Now Maeve was on her own. She supposed she'd see Deirdre from time to time, but they would be more like neighbours than sisters. Of course, Maeve still had her parents, but that was little comfort. If her mother spoke to Maeve at all, it was to assign her a chore or scold her. As for her father, Maeve barely saw him. He spent his days in the smithy and the field. He came in for meals, but it was only to eat. As soon as the food was gone, he left again. He spoke so seldom, Maeve sometimes wondered if he knew how.

In the weeks following Deirdre's marriage, Maeve wandered through her days in a fog. She did her chores and ate her meals, but when she put her head down each night, she was hard pressed to remember any of it.

"Take these eggs to the village and don't break them," her mother said as she slid the basket over Maeve's arm. "We need the coin they'll bring."

Maeve nodded. "Yes, Ma." And then, because she wasn't sure that was the correct response, she added, "No, Ma, I won't break them."

With her lips pressed together in a tight line, her mother shook her head and shooed her out the door. "Off with you then. And mind you bring home every penny."

With Deirdre gone, Maeve had thought her mother's attitude toward her might soften. But if anything, she seemed to lose her temper with Maeve more readily. Deirdre had once told Maeve that their mother had been bedridden for weeks after giving birth to Maeve. And she was told she would never again bear a child. Not only that, but Maeve had been a small baby and sickly too. Though Deirdre had only been a child herself at the time, she swore Maeve cried non-stop for the first three years of her life. Maeve wondered if her mother had never forgiven her for that.

In the village, Maeve looked about for Declan. He was rarely there when she arrived but would show up after. This day was no exception.

"Will you come to the Druid camp this afternoon?" he asked her.

"Do you want me to?" she replied coyly. Declan often invited her to visit the camp these days. Though she assumed he asked her because he liked her, he had yet to say so.

He seemed to be giving her question a great deal of thought. Finally he said, "It feels right to have you there."

Maeve was learning that Declan could be maddeningly evasive, speaking in riddles that could be interpreted a number of ways. She didn't even try to work out which meaning he intended. She sighed and nodded. "First I have to sell my eggs."

"I'll help you."

Before Maeve realized what he was doing, he grabbed three eggs in each hand and began darting about the village square, hawking them like a proper vendor. At first she was embarrassed by his forwardness. But when the number of eggs started to dwindle, she was pleased. They would have more of the afternoon to spend together.

———

Their walk through the forest was over too soon, and Maeve was sad to think her time alone with Declan had come to an end. It wasn't that she didn't want to be among the Druids. She always looked forward to speaking with Bradan and laughing with Enda, but part of her would have been happy to keep walking.

When they entered the clearing, she smiled and waved to all the Druids, who she now knew quite well.

"Come," Declan said. "Bradan will want to speak with you."

Maeve looked toward the log where the old man usually sat, but he wasn't there. Declan seemed to know where to find him though, so Maeve followed. To her surprise, he led her into the woodland on the far side of the meadow. The trees were closer together here, blocking the cheerful autumn sun. Maeve shivered, but not only because of the chill. There was something else. It was as if the air was clawing at her, trying to get inside. She pulled her shawl tight and tried to push the unsettling feeling away. It was foolishness. She wouldn't think about it. She would concentrate on following Declan.

They made their way in silence. Caught up in her thoughts, Maeve didn't know how long they'd been walking, but finally Declan stopped.

"Right about here, I think," he murmured more to himself than her.

Maeve looked around. She could see only forest. There *was* only forest. Whatever had unsettled her was gone. Her uneasiness fell away, and she silently scolded herself for letting her imagination get the better of her.

She looked up into the treetops. A web of green all but blotted out the sky. She was sad to see the leaves of the alders and oaks already turning colour.

"Autumn is beginning," she sighed.

Declan followed her gaze. "Yes. In the days following the celebration of Alban Elfed, the signs of autumn are everywhere."

Maeve regarded him curiously. "What is Alban Elfed?"

"The fall equinox. A celebration of the changing of the seasons."

"But I don't want summer to end," Maeve said. "I love the warmth and the sun and the flowers. Why would I want rain and cold to take its place? You Druids have very strange ideas."

Declan chuckled. "All of life is a cycle—the weather, the changes in light, the growing and harvesting seasons. These are repeated over and over in nature as well as in our own lives." He shrugged. "It is the way of nature, so of course we celebrate it."

Maeve thought about that. Druids were so accepting of life. How she envied them. She peered through the trees again and asked, "Why have we stopped?" Before Declan could answer, she saw Bradan. Had he stepped out from behind a tree, or had he been standing in plain sight the whole time? His dark mantle made him melt into the forest. If it weren't for the white of his beard, Maeve might not have seen him at all.

The old man smiled and stretched out a wrinkled hand to her. His touch was cool, and though Maeve had thought him frail, his grip was firm. "Welcome, young Maeve," he said, releasing her hand. "Come and walk with me." He turned and started moving deeper into the forest.

Maeve glanced apprehensively at Declan.

"Go," he said quietly. "I shall wait for you in the meadow."

"You come too," she urged him.

"I shall wait for you in the meadow," he said again, then turned and left her.

Chapter 4

Though Maeve had been reluctant to follow Bradan deeper into the trees, her misgivings left her once they began to walk.

"Open yourself to it," Bradan told her.

Maeve regarded him curiously. "To what?"

"The forest is calling to you. You can hear it, but you aren't listening."

Maeve looked skyward. *Why must Druids always speak in riddles?* "I don't understand," she said crossly. "You talk in circles. I can't even find the beginning of your meaning, let alone the end."

The old man smiled. "You know more than you realize, child. You need only draw back the curtain in your mind." Then he laughed, and the music of it wound itself round the trees.

"Are you teasing me?" Maeve demanded.

He sighed and shook his head. "No, child. Quite the opposite. I am envious of you. Life has not yet jaded you."

"Is that a good thing?"

He seemed to think about that. "Yes and no."

Why couldn't he give her a clear answer? Maeve growled and kicked a pine cone. Bradan leaned wearily on his walking stick and placed a hand on her shoulder. She turned to look at him, and he smoothed away her frown.

28

"Your innocence allows you to see things as they are and not with a preconceived notion of what you think they are. It allows you to look with your heart."

"And that's good?"

"It is."

"Before, you said it was good *and* bad. What is the bad part?"

"Innocence can make you a victim."

"Of what?"

"There are people less kind, less honest— people concerned only with themselves. They sometimes take advantage of the guileless."

"Are you innocent?" Maeve asked bluntly.

Bradan's eyebrows shot up. When they relaxed again, he said, "No. I haven't been for some time, I'm afraid. Innocence is mostly reserved for the young."

"Are you jaded then?"

He cleared his throat and shook his head. "No, not jaded. But I recognize those who are. It comes from having lived a long life. I still see with my heart, but I also see with my head. It is a balance."

For the first time, Maeve thought she understood what Bradan meant. It was like coming in out of a heavy rain and slipping off her sodden mantle.

He swept his hand through the air. "Never mind that now. Tell me what you have been doing since last you were here."

She shrugged. "The same as always. Chores. Feeding the chickens. Gathering firewood. Scrubbing pans." She gestured to the forest surrounding them. "Coming here is my only pleasure."

He tapped his head with a gnarled finger. "And what about up here? Do you not find pleasure in your thoughts?"

A fire flared inside Maeve.

She scowled. "I hate it when you ask about my thoughts. They aren't pleasant at all. They make no sense, and they keep me from concentrating on my work. I wish they would go away. No one else thinks strange things."

Maeve knew she was being churlish, but lately even the smallest thing could set her off. Since Deirdre's marriage, life at home had become intolerable. Now she had Deirdre's chores as well as her own, and her mother had less patience than ever—if that were possible.

She felt more like a servant than a daughter, and it was all she could do to squelch the hurt. It was like walking on fragile ice; at any moment she might crash through and drown in her own emotions. Since she couldn't tell her parents how she felt, she was forced to find other means of release—shouting her anger into the wind, complaining to the farm animals, kicking inanimate objects. And now lashing out at Bradan.

The old man made his way to a moss-covered boulder and sat down. "Ah, that's better." He patted the rock. "Come and sit for a moment, child." When Maeve dropped down beside him, he said, "Look around and tell me what you see."

It seemed a strange request, but Maeve obliged. "I see trees, some very tall, some small. I see bushes and rotting logs, fallen cones and needles on the ground, wisps of grass, dirt and stones." She shrugged. "That's all. I know the sky is above the trees, but I can't really see it."

As she spoke, Bradan nodded, and when she was finished, he said, "Now close your eyes and look again."

Maeve regarded him skeptically. "How can I look if my eyes are closed?"

"Try," he said.

"But—"

"Try."

With a frustrated growl, Maeve closed her eyes and made herself imagine the scene she'd been staring at.

After a moment, Bradan said, "What do you see now?"

"The same as before, but it's blurry." She opened her eyes. "Bradan, why am I doing this?"

"Close your eyes," he told her. When she had, he said, "It's blurry because you are relying on your memory to see it."

Maeve's eyes flew open again. "Well of course I am!" she said. "What else can I do when my eyes are closed? I can't see through my eyelids."

"Close your eyes," Bradan said again, more sternly this time. "And keep them closed."

Once more she did as he bade her, though she was becoming more than a little agitated by his orders. Whatever this game was, she didn't like it.

"When you look at the forest this time, Maeve, I want you to open yourself to it. Let it come to you. Experience it, not with your eyes but with your entire being. What can you hear?"

"Nothing," Maeve replied obstinately.

"Nothing?" He turned the word back on her. "Nonsense. In your mind, walk among the trees."

"Why?" she demanded.

Ignoring her, he repeated his instruction. "Walk among the trees."

"Fine," she grumbled. "I'm walking."

"Are you on a path?"

"Yes."

"What is under your feet?"

"Hardened earth, bits of rotting wood, pine cones, pine needles, dry leaves."

"Walk on them and tell me what you hear."

Though it seemed a pointless exercise, Maeve did as he said. Gazing into her mind's eye, she watched herself move along the forest path.

Then the strangest thing happened. After a few steps she realized she was no longer watching. It was as if she were really there. She could feel the muscles of her legs tighten and relax. She could feel her feet push against the spongy ground, the ragged gorse slide through her fingers, and her shawl catch on a branch. She was becoming one with the forest. She was inside it, and it was inside her. Her whole being surged with energy as if the trees had parted and the sun was filling her with light.

"Well?" Bradan said.

Without opening her eyes, she marvelled, "I'm here. The forest is all around me. It's as if it has swallowed me. I'm touching it and it's touching me. I feel the leaves crunch and the twigs snap as I walk, and I feel ground beneath my step. There's a small stone in my shoe, and it's pushing into my foot." She wiggled her foot as if to dislodge the stone and then continued. "The bushes rustle as I push past, and a breeze sighs through the tree-tops. A bird flies so near my head I can hear its wings beat the air."

She opened her eyes and blinked with amazement as she realized that she'd had sensations like these before. She had visited places without ever taking a step and had done things without actually doing them, but never intentionally. These experiences had always scared her. This time, though, she'd been in control. She'd walked through the forest inside her mind on purpose. Maeve felt relieved and exhilarated, like a small child who had just taken her first steps.

Bradan smiled. "Good. Now close your eyes again and go back. Breathe the forest in. What can you smell?"

———

When Bradan and Maeve emerged from the trees, Declan was sitting on the grass, whittling a sturdy stick of blackthorn.

"A new staff for you, Master Bradan," he said, jumping up and offering the stick to the old man. To Maeve he said, "It's getting late. We should go."

Maeve nodded and opened her mouth to reply but was distracted by someone waving and shouting from across the meadow.

It was Enda. "Maeve!"

Maeve grinned and returned Enda's wave. "I'll be right back," she said to Declan, excusing herself and running to greet her friend.

They collided in a hug and an eruption of laughter.

"I didn't think I'd see you today," Maeve said. "Declan told me you were gathering herbs."

"Indeed I was," Enda replied, her cheeks as plump and rosy as two ripe apples. "I have something for you." She rummaged through her basket and came out clutching a bouquet. "Meadowsweet," she explained, running her hand over the clusters of small white flowers. She thrust them under Maeve's nose.

"Lovely," Maeve said, inhaling the sweet fragrance.

"Take them. If you scatter the blossoms over the floor of your cottage, it will smell ever so good when you walk on them. Brewed into a tea, it can settle a queasy stomach."

Maeve put the flowers into her basket. "Thank

you, Enda. I am most grateful. Now I should go. My mother will be wondering where I am."

The two exchanged hugs once more, and Maeve turned back toward Declan. But he wasn't where she'd left him. A quick look around showed her that he had already begun the stroll across the meadow toward her part of the forest. Bradan was with him, and they were deep in conversation. She loped toward them and, not wishing to interrupt, fell in step behind.

Lifting one of the flower clusters from her basket, she inhaled its fragrance and sighed happily. Once again the afternoon with the Druids had replaced the oppressive clouds in her life with sunshine. Maeve knew she was late and her mother would be cross, but she would think of an excuse. For the moment, she was content to be swinging her basket and strolling across the Druid meadow.

She wasn't trying to listen to the conversation between Declan and Bradan, and she would have had no idea what they were talking about if it weren't for a sudden gust of wind that tore the flower from her hand and swept the old man's words into her ears.

"You've done well, lad," he said. "You were right to bring her to me."

CHAPTER 5

Maeve couldn't recall precisely when she and Declan left Bradan behind and entered the forest, nor could she remember if she bid the old man farewell. Her mind was too busy trying to make sense of what he'd said—*"You were right to bring her to me."*

What did that mean? It sounded like a ruse. Maeve thought Declan had taken her to the Druid camp because he wanted her to know how he lived. She had thought he liked her.

Now she was sure there was an altogether different reason for him to have taken her there. She realized how gullible she'd been. And she was angry. Declan had no right to manipulate her.

"Maeve. Maeve!" Declan clamped a hand on her arm. "Slow down," he laughed. "You're not that late."

Jolted from her thoughts, Maeve pulled her arm free and whirled on him. "How dare you!" she shouted, her eyebrows knotted in rage.

Declan blinked at her and then at his hand as he took a step back. "I'm sorry," he said. "Did I hurt you? I didn't think I was holding your arm that tightly. I was only trying to get you to slow down."

Maeve clucked her tongue. "I'm not talking about that."

Declan frowned. "Then what? What's the matter?"

She moved toward him and snarled through gritted teeth. "I heard you and Bradan talking about me. Bradan said you were right to bring me to him. What did he mean?"

Maeve could see Declan was searching for the right words, but she was not going to allow him to put her off with a riddle. Not this time.

"Tell me the truth, Declan. Is Bradan the reason you've been taking me to your camp?"

Declan didn't reply, but Maeve could see the answer on his face. It was like a knife cutting into her. She stepped back.

"Why?" she said, trying to keep the hurt from her voice.

"I'm sorry," Declan replied. He looked down at his feet, up at the sky and finally at the trees around him. The only place he didn't look was at Maeve. "It's true. I did want you and Bradan to meet. More than that I cannot say."

"Why?" Maeve demanded again, pushing away her pain with anger. "Why must you always put me off? I deserve an answer!"

His unsteady gaze met her fierce one. "And you shall get it. I promise. Soon." He pointed in the direction from which they'd come. "I should get back. And you need to get home."

And with that, he left her.

Declan was right about one thing, Maeve thought as she watched him rush away. She did need to get home. She swiped at the tears rolling down her cheeks. She should hurry, but discovering the truth had snuffed out her anger and sucked the energy from her. It was all she could do to put one foot in front of the other, and because of that it took her three times as long as it should have to walk the remaining distance to the cottage.

As soon as she saw her mother standing in the dooryard, she sensed she was in trouble. The closer she got, the more wary she became. The murderous expression on her mother's face would have caused Far Dorcha—the dark creature— to run and hide. But Maeve knew running wouldn't save her. When she was but a step away, she stopped.

Before she could blink, her mother's hand shot out, cuffing her so hard it sent her staggering.

Maeve shielded her head with her arms.

"Where have you been?" her mother growled, advancing on her.

"In the village, selling the eggs," she whimpered. "I'm sorry I'm late. It took a long time today."

A resounding smack set Maeve's ears ringing.

"Don't lie to me, girl. Do you take me for a fool? Agnes from down the way was in the village and saw you with a Druid boy. She says you went into the woods with him." She lunged at Maeve again, catching her with a slap to her cheek and ear. "Where is your head? Did you think no one would see? Did you think I wouldn't find out? How long have you been sneaking around?"

38

"I haven't been. It's not what you think, Ma!" Maeve cried and began fumbling inside her basket for the money she'd collected. "See, Ma?" she said, holding out the handful of coins. "I have the money. Every penny, just like you told me."

Her mother swatted her hand away and the coins flew into the air. "You stupid girl!" she spat the words at her. "Do you think a few coins can save you? You've been up to no good, and you've been caught. Not only are you stupid, but you can't be trusted." Angrily she batted Maeve one way and then the other.

"Stop, Ma, stop!" Maeve wailed. "Please. I've not done wrong. Yes, I walked with Declan, but—"

"So that's his name, is it—Declan?" She boxed Maeve's ears again.

Maeve tried to break free but her mother had an iron grip on her arm, and no matter how she squirmed, she couldn't get loose.

"Please, Ma," Maeve wept. "He's my friend. That's all. I swear!"

Writhing to free herself, she caught a glimpse of her father standing at the door to the smithy. She thought he must have heard her cries and had left his work to save her from her mother's tirade, but all he did was stand there, watching.

Her mother twisted her arm, and Maeve cried out in pain.

"Enough!" a voice boomed behind her. Maeve was locked in her mother's grip and couldn't see who it was. "Let the girl go."

Maeve's mother stopped twisting her arm but didn't release her. "Mind your business, old man," she snarled. "This is a family matter."

"I said let her go."

It was Bradan. Maeve had no doubt. No one else spoke with such authority. She was glad he'd come, but what was he doing here?

She felt her mother's grip ease, and then the woman spun her around and shoved her toward Bradan. Reeling out of control, Maeve would have slammed hard into the old man, but Declan leaped forward and caught her just in time.

"Are you all right?" he asked, holding her up, for her knees had forsaken her.

Maeve nodded and bit her lip, trying to control her weeping. She was embarrassed for Declan to see her this way.

"Are you certain?" Bradan asked, his gaze assessing her injuries.

Maeve sniffed and nodded and rubbed her arm.

Frowning, the Druid turned his attention to Maeve's mother. "It is fortunate the lad and I arrived when we did, though that is not what brought us here." He gestured to Maeve's father, who still stood at the door of the smithy. "I have business with you and your husband."

Maeve's mother's eyes narrowed. "What business?"

Without realizing, Maeve leaned toward Bradan. She too was curious to know what he wanted with her parents.

"I shall speak with both you and your husband, if you please," Bradan replied.

"Eamon!" Maeve's mother beckoned her husband. To Maeve, she said, "Get in the cottage. I shall deal with you later."

Maeve started to move, but Bradan put a hand on her arm.

"No." He shook his head. "This concerns the girl. She will stay."

"Well, get on with it then," Maeve's mother grumbled, her husband now by her side.

Bradan acknowledged the other man with a nod.

As her father returned the gesture, Maeve noted a wary gleam in his eyes. It was almost as if he knew what Bradan had come about. But that was impossible. How could he know? She didn't have time to give the matter any thought because Bradan had begun to speak.

"From the scene I witnessed as I arrived"—he cleared his throat meaningfully—"I am inclined to believe you know that the lad here"—he gestured to Declan—"has been visiting Maeve in the village when she sells eggs."

"He's been doing more than that," Maeve's mother muttered.

Bradan continued as if she hadn't spoken. "The lad sensed there was something special about Maeve."

"What d'ya mean?" Eamon eyed the old Druid suspiciously.

41

"The boy suspected she has the gift of sight."

Maeve gasped. *What was Bradan saying?* The only gift she had was for daydreaming her way into trouble.

"The gift of sight, is it?" Maeve's mother hooted. "I always knew she was funny in the head, that one." She snickered and elbowed her husband, but instead of chortling too, he narrowed his eyes and stared harder at Bradan.

Bradan continued. "When Declan told me about her, I asked him to bring her to me so that I could determine her abilities for myself. That is why she has been visiting our camp."

"I didn't know, I swear!" Maeve exclaimed when her mother shot her a threatening glare. "I thought Declan was being friendly is all."

"And," Bradan pushed on, "I am pleased to say the lad was right. Maeve does indeed have the gift. She is a seer."

"Codswallop!" her mother said. "The girl is strange—there's no denying that—but she's no seer. How could she be? She's not even a Druid."

"Sometimes cuckoos lay their eggs in other birds' nests," Bradan said quietly.

The colour drained from Eamon's face.

Maeve was confused. Bradan was speaking in riddles again, and she had no idea what he was talking about. But it seemed her father did, and judging from the look of him, Bradan's words didn't sit well.

"Druid or not, she has the gift," Bradan said.

Maeve's mother leaned toward Bradan and tapped her head. "I think your brain is addled, old man. You're not making any sense."

Bradan sighed. "Let me speak plainly. I have a proposition for you. If Maeve agrees—and you as her parents also agree—I would like to take Maeve on as my apprentice."

Maeve was so stunned all she could do was blink at Bradan.

"What's that mean?" Her mother was suddenly wary.

"It means she would come and live among the Druids, and I would teach her how to use her gift."

"She has to live with you Druids?"

Bradan nodded.

"Can she come home to do her chores?"

He shook his head. "Her life with you would be done—as if she had left to marry."

"What's in it for us then? Are you going to pay us?"

"The girl is not a cow or pig to be sold at market, and Druids are not merchants. If Maeve joins us, she will be fed and clothed and cared for. She will become one of us and adopt Druid ways. She will be encouraged to pursue knowledge and revere nature. And she will learn to use her gift to help others. You, as her parents, could be very proud."

"Proud!" Maeve's mother snorted. "Proud doesn't get the pots scrubbed, the fire tended and the water fetched. You are asking us to give over the girl and get nothing in return."

Bradan shook his head. "I am asking you to act in the girl's best interest. Let her choose."

All eyes turned to Maeve, and she caught her breath in surprise. She had never been given a choice about anything in her life, and she could tell by her mother's piercing glare that she wasn't being given one now. Her mother was holding her tongue in the old Druid's presence because she feared his power and influence. Once he was gone, her true nature would surface once more.

Maeve's gaze darted nervously round the group. Everyone was expecting her to say something. But what? For the first time in her life, her mind was as empty as a starless night sky.

CHAPTER 6

It was agreed that Maeve and her parents would discuss Bradan's offer, and he would return the next day for their answer. Before he took his leave, though, the seer made it clear that Maeve's parents were not to lay a finger on her or they would pay dearly for it. Maeve couldn't think what the punishment might be, but she knew her parents recognized Druid authority and would heed Bradan's warning. It didn't cool her mother's anger, but it meant she could only show it through threatening looks and harsh words—instead of the back of her hand.

Maeve scurried silently about the cottage, tending to her chores and trying to stay out of her mother's way. When it was time to eat, she ran to the smithy to fetch her father and then quietly took her place at the table.

She stared at the food in front of her. She knew her parents were watching, but she didn't dare return their gaze. In their present mood they might take it as insolence. No, it was best to make herself as invisible as possible, so she focused on eating and retreated into her mind.

Bradan had said the decision was to be Maeve's, but she knew it wouldn't be. Her mother decided things. It had always been that way, and an old man suggesting otherwise wasn't going to make it so.

According to Bradan, Maeve had the gift of sight. How could he know that merely by speaking with her a few times? She didn't see how that was possible. He said he wanted to take her on as an apprentice! The prospect sent Maeve into a panic. What if she accepted his offer and it turned out he was wrong and she *didn't* have the gift? What if she was exactly what everyone had always said she was—a strange girl who spent her time daydreaming? Would he send her back to her parents? And what if they wouldn't have her? If the Druids threw her out and her parents disowned her, she would have no one to care for her and nowhere to live. Maybe she was better off continuing as she was.

But what if she *was* a seer? Bradan was confident enough in her ability that he wanted to teach her. If his efforts were successful, her wild imaginings might finally make sense. She would master her thoughts once and for all, and she would learn to interpret the visions of others too, because that was what seers did. Then folk would seek her out. She would be respected and accepted. Wasn't that what she wanted?

"We'd best be thinking what to do." Her mother's hard voice cut into Maeve's thoughts and she looked up. But of course, her mother wasn't speaking to her. Her gaze was fixed on her husband, who was concentrating on his supper.

When he went on eating, she swatted his arm. "Have you gone deaf, man? I said we need to decide what to do with the girl."

He shrugged, and without looking up from his bowl he said, "What does it matter? If she wants to go, let her."

"Who'll do her chores?"

Her husband shrugged again. "You."

"Me?" she cried. "I have enough to do already!"

"You're always saying the girl is slow and gets things wrong. Where's the help in that? Maybe you'd do better without her."

Maeve blinked in amazement. She had never heard her father string so many words together at one time. And awful words they were too. She had always thought him a quiet man who liked her well enough but preferred his own company. Now she realized she didn't know him at all. The truth, it seemed, was that he had no more affection for her than did her mother. The only difference was that he seldom had to deal with her. His work took him to the smithy and the field. Maeve's mother tended to domestic matters.

Catching her mother's gaze drifting toward her, Maeve quickly looked back at the table.

"Hmmmm," the woman said thoughtfully. "What you say is true, husband. The girl is a poor worker, to be sure. I have to keep after her all the time. And—not that anyone would want her—in a few months she could marry and she'd be gone anyway." Without warning, she shot her husband

47

a startled look. "Hold on—if no one weds her, we could be lumbered with her forever!"

"There you are then," Maeve's father said as he pushed his empty bowl away. "Let the Druid have her. Good riddance, I say."

"I suppose. Still and all, I think he owes us something. If the old fool thinks she has value, he should give over a few coins."

"Considerin' how much trouble the girl is, maybe we should be payin' him," her father said, sending the pair into gales of laughter.

Maeve couldn't believe her parents would be so cruel. Without thinking, she raised her voice so she could be heard above their guffaws. "What if I don't want to go with the Druids?"

Immediately her parents' laughter dried up and they stared at her in disbelief. Then faster than Maeve could blink, her mother sprang up and leaned across the table.

"Mind your tongue, girl," she bellowed as she raised her hand.

Maeve cringed, waiting for the slap she knew was coming, but her father caught his wife's arm before she could deliver the blow.

"Don't be stupid, woman. You heard the Druid," he snapped at her. "He might be an old man, but he holds sway with kings. If he suspects you've touched the girl, we're done for. Of that you can be sure."

Buoyed by the notion that her father would save her from a beating—even if his reasons had nothing to do with her welfare—Maeve dared to speak again. "Bradan said the decision was to be mine, but you haven't even asked me what I want."

"It matters not what the Druid said," her mother growled. "He's not here, is he? And it matters not what you want either. You will do what I say!"

There was a long silence as Maeve's parents glared at her. She considered her options. There weren't many. She could beg her parents to let her stay—for all the good it would do—or she could surrender herself to the fact that they were going to hand her over to Bradan in the morning. It was no choice really.

Then a spark of defiance—something Maeve had felt from time to time in her life but never acted upon—flared inside her. This *would* be her decision. Not her parents'. Not Bradan's either. She wouldn't stay where she wasn't wanted; nor would she go where she didn't belong.

She pushed back the bench and rose to her feet. Then pulling herself up as tall as she could, she collected her shawl and moved to the cottage entrance. When she got to the door, she paused and looked back.

"Good-bye, Ma. Good-bye, Pa," she said without emotion. "You'll not be troubled by me again."

CHAPTER 7

Maeve thought her parents would chase after her and punish her for her impudence. But she'd already reached the road when her mother appeared in the cottage entrance. Instead of screaming at Maeve, she spat on the ground and shut the door.

So that was that. Maeve's time with her parents had come to an end. As the realization sank in, her confidence wavered. It had been her decision to leave, but now that it was done, she couldn't undo it.

She took a last look at the small, round, wattle-and-daub cottage with its heather roof. Her gaze travelled to the dooryard—the chickens scratching the hard dirt, the embers of the cooking fire smouldering under a layer of white ash, the wedding pig snuffling for food scraps in a nearby pen. At the smithy entrance a wooden bucket sat beside a trough, waiting for Maeve to fill it with water from the stream. Not tonight, she thought. Not any night ever again.

Maeve turned away and stepped into the long yellow grass leading to the forest.

Was she sad? Perhaps. A part of her life was ending. Was she relieved? She supposed she was that as well. Her mother had beaten her for the last time. That was something to be thankful for. More than anything else, though, Maeve was numb. It was hard to believe the only home she had ever known was now lost to her, and she was well and truly on her own.

She supposed she should make her way to the Druid camp, but she hesitated. Bradan had said the choice was hers but he really hadn't given her a choice. He had to have known her parents would wash their hands of her, leaving the Druid camp the only other place she could go.

But did she want to?

Bradan and Declan had misled her. They had taken advantage of her naivety in order to study her. They had mistreated her just as surely as her parents had. Declan had feigned friendship, and Bradan had dug into her mind. *How was that better?* It seemed to Maeve that if she joined the Druids, she would be jumping from one fire into another.

But what else could she do? It wasn't as if a neighbour would help her. Most folks' lives were hard enough without taking on a foolish girl whose own parents couldn't abide her. Maeve had no friends either. She'd thought Declan was her friend, but she'd been wrong.

What about Deirdre? Perhaps she would take Maeve in. They were sisters after all. Maeve took a deep breath and squared her shoulders. There was only one way to find out.

Deirdre's new home was on the other side of

the village. The quickest way was through the village, but Maeve had never been to the village in the evening, and she didn't want to draw attention to herself, so she kept to the woods.

She wasn't certain where Deirdre's new home was, never having been to it, but she had an inkling where it should be. As it turned out, the problem was solved for her because at the first farm she came to, Deirdre was standing in the dooryard feeding the chickens.

"Sister!" Maeve called.

Deirdre looked up, but as Maeve ran toward her, she went back to scattering chicken feed.

"Deirdre," Maeve panted and smiled when she reached her. "It's good to see you. You look well."

"Why are you here?" Deirdre frowned and dumped out the last of the feed. "It is late. Is something amiss? Did Ma send you?"

Maeve was taken aback. She hadn't expected her sister to be so cold. "No. I mean yes." She shook her head to clear it. "No, Ma didn't send me, but yes, something is amiss."

"What?"

Her sister was clearly not interested in small talk, so Maeve got straight to the point. "I've left home."

Deirdre didn't seem surprised. "They threw you out."

"No!" Maeve protested. "It was my choosing." She didn't add that her parents would have sent her away if she hadn't left.

"Why have you come here?"

"I need somewhere to stay—only until..." Maeve faltered, realizing she had no idea how long she might need Deirdre's help.

"Not here." Her sister shook her head. "There's no room. We're already six people, and it's a small cottage. We're on top of one another as it is and" —she touched her belly—"soon enough there will be seven."

"But I—I..." Maeve stammered.

"There's no room I tell you, so you'd best be on your way. I still have chores to tend to." With that she started to walk away. But at the entrance to an outbuilding, she looked back and said, "Good luck to you, sister."

———

Maeve left the farm in a daze and headed back into the forest, deeper and deeper, until she no longer knew where she was. The forest had always been her refuge, the place she went when her spirits needed lifting—but not this evening. She barely saw the trees she was picking her way around. She just walked—and tried not to think.

So without her noticing, evening turned to night. It wasn't until she stumbled over a tree root and nearly fell that she became aware of how dark it was. The forest, so many shades of green by day, had become a blur of wadded grays.

Maeve pulled her shawl tightly about her. Though it had been a warm day, the night was turning cold. She needed to find shelter out of the elements—a hollow log or a gully perhaps.

She scanned her immediate surroundings, but seeing nothing suitable, she kept moving. Finally, squinting into the growing gloom, she spied a rock embankment and started toward it. Perhaps it would provide shelter.

She felt her way along the base of the towering rock wall, searching for a crevice large enough to crawl into, but all the spaces she found were much too small—and then the wall ended.

Or did it?

Maeve followed the rock wall around a corner, and to her surprise it carried on. It was already quite dark, but as she moved forward the heavy greyness turned to black. Maeve looked up. The stars were gone. She must be under an overhang of some sort.

Pushing on, she realized she was walking downhill, and her imagination started up again. What if the ground suddenly fell away and she tumbled into a pit and couldn't get out? So deep in the forest, she wouldn't be found. She could die here! Perhaps she should stop. Perhaps she should spend the night where she was. If it rained or the wind came up, she would be protected here. Yet part of her was curious to find out what lay ahead. She wished she had a torch—or at least a candle to light her way.

As if wishing was all she need do, she was instantly able to see through the darkness. She knew she was only imagining what lay ahead, but her heart sped up. Bradan said she had the gift of sight. Was this a vision? Was she seeing what actually lay ahead? With all her being, she concentrated on the images forming before her.

She saw that she was in a tunnel which ran a fair distance before opening into a large cave, empty save for a small stream of water that trickled down one wall and then out through a fissure in the rock. Maeve blinked and the cave vanished. It was once again black as pitch.

But the cave had been so real, just as the forest had been when Bradan had told her to walk through it with her eyes closed. If her mind was showing her something that truly existed and she really was in a tunnel, there should be another wall. Maeve stretched out her arms and began moving sideways. It must be a very wide tunnel, she decided after several seconds of shuffling. Unless it wasn't a tunnel at all. She looked up. The stars were still hidden, so there was definitely a roof of some sort blotting them out. She continued shambling sideways, and at last her fingers touched cool, smooth rock again.

She was so relieved, she laughed. She *was* in a tunnel. She hadn't imagined it; she had seen it. That meant the cave must be real too. She pictured it in her mind once more. There was nothing exceptional about it, nothing to draw her to it, and yet Maeve sensed it had been shown to her for a reason. So she continued moving toward it.

CHAPTER 8

When the ground levelled out, Maeve knew she had reached the cave. She felt her way around the rock until she came to the trickle of water. She followed its course down the wall, and when she found the fissure where it disappeared again, she grinned and hugged herself. Though she couldn't see through the darkness, she knew the cave was exactly as it had appeared in her mind. Maybe Bradan was right. Maybe she did have the gift of sight.

Using the wall to guide her, she moved to the far side and lowered herself to the floor.

Only then did she remember the circumstances that had brought her here, and her sense of well-being melted away like wax from a lighted candle. Her parents' dismissal of her was no more than she would have expected, but it hurt nonetheless. She hadn't expected Deirdre to turn her away, though, and that hurt more. Then there was Bradan and Declan. They had plotted behind her back. How could she trust them now? Round and round her thoughts whirled as if caught in a windstorm. But no matter how much she thought on the situation, she couldn't settle on what to do.

She cleared the cave floor around her of small stones and other debris and stretched out on the ground. It was hard. She wished she'd thought to soften it with pine boughs, but she was too tired to bother now. She shivered. She might be protected from wind and rain, but there was still a chill in the air. She wrapped herself in her shawl, lay her head on her arm and closed her eyes. Perhaps a plan would come to her in her dreams.

Maeve had been deep asleep, but now she was not. She wasn't awake, but neither was she truly sleeping. The weary part of her seemed to know it wasn't yet morning and struggled to slip back into peaceful oblivion, but her practical side pushed its way toward consciousness.

She was hot—so hot she was sweating. Her clothes were sticking to her, and her skin was slick. How was that possible? It had been cool when she'd arrived at the cave, and the night should be getting colder, not warmer.

She took a deep breath and instantly regretted it as a horrid odour invaded her senses. She wrinkled her nose against it. She couldn't identify it. All she knew was that it hadn't been there when she'd gone to sleep.

Had she been ill? If she'd thrown up, that would account for the terrible smell. Had her trek through the forest in the cool evening been too much? She didn't feel sick—no upset stomach, no achiness. She was only hot, as if she'd been standing over the cooking fire for too long.

She rolled onto her back and threw off the shawl. The heat—and the smell—continued. Both seemed to be coming in waves. She put a hand to her face and felt hot air sliding over her skin. This strange warmth wasn't coming from inside her. It was—

Maeve's eyes flew open, and she found herself staring into two yellow eyes, each the size of her head. She blinked. Her imagination must be playing tricks on her. A rush of hot, foul air streamed over her face, causing her eyelids to flutter.

She wasn't imagining *that*.

Digging her heels into the hard ground, she pushed away from the eyes. But they moved with her—following her. Maeve backed up again. The eyes stayed with her. So it went until she could retreat no farther. She had reached the wall.

Then she did the only thing she could think of. She screamed.

Instantly the eyes were replaced by darkness, but only for a moment. When they returned there was a fire in them that hadn't been there before.

Frightened and panicked, Maeve screamed again, and again the eyes vanished.

"*Must you shriek?*" demanded a voice in her head—but it wasn't her voice. Startled, Maeve swallowed the next scream forming in her throat. "*You are hurting my ears.*"

"What?" Maeve was completely confused.

"*I said, your shrieking hurts my ears.*"

Incredulous, Maeve stared at the eyes. They blinked. "*Is that you talking?*" she thought to them.

The eyes moved up and down.

"*You spoke to me?*"

"*I did.*"

Maeve was more baffled than ever. "*But how? You haven't said a word.*"

The eyes became yellow slits. "*Nor have you.*"

It was true, Maeve realized. She was carrying on a conversation with—something—without either of them uttering a sound. How could that be?

The creature stood. At least, Maeve assumed it did. The cave was so dark she couldn't make out its shape, but its eyes climbed upward, and they were now regarding her from a great height. Whatever this creature was, it was gigantic, and if she angered it, she sensed it could crush her in an instant.

Realizing how vulnerable she was, Maeve sat up, pressed her body tightly against the cave wall and drew her knees close. "*Who are you?*" she thought fearfully to the creature. "*What are you? All I can see are your eyes.*"

The creature chuckled silently. "*Surely you've heard of dragons.*"

Maeve gasped and tried to push herself through the cave wall. "*You're a dragon?*"

"*Riasc Tiarna, Lord of the Marshes.*" The creature seemed to grow taller with this declaration. "*And you are trespassing.*"

"*I-I-I am?*" she stuttered.

The great yellow eyes moved up and down.

"*This is your cave?*"

"*All caves in this land are mine.*"

"*I'm sorry,*" Maeve said. "*I—I didn't know.*"

As she watched, the dragon's eyes vanished into the darkness, there was a loud scraping sound and the floor beneath her shuddered. Then the whole cave began to shake—and Maeve with it. It wasn't until it settled again, and Riasc Tiarna's yellow eyes were once more staring at her, that Maeve realized he had taken himself to the far side of the cave and sat down.

"*What do you want from me?*" she thought.

"*No need to be afraid, young Maeve,*" the voice in her head replied.

Maeve was surprised. "*How do you know my name?*"

"*Your mind is unguarded,*" came back the reply. "*Anyone can look into it.*"

"*That may be, but I don't walk about thinking my name. Yet you know it. How?*"

Inside her head the dragon chuckled again. "*Not a great deal escapes my notice. I have known of you for some time. I knew you would make your way here this night.*"

"*How could you?*"

The dragon didn't reply, and though he had told her she needn't be afraid, his silence did little to ease her misgivings. He was bigger and more powerful than she was, and he had the advantage of surprise. She was supposed to be a seer, yet she hadn't had the slightest hint she was going to be awakened from a sound sleep by a dragon.

Still, he hadn't harmed her—at least not yet.

"*What do you want from me*?" she asked again.

Maeve waited for the dragon to fill her mind with some fantastic demand or task, but her head remained quiet. She peered through the darkness of the cave into his hypnotic gaze.

When a minute passed and he still hadn't replied, her trepidation gave way to impatience. "*Well*?"

He sighed so deeply that even from the other side of the cave, his hot breath washed over her and set her sweating again.

"*Could you not do that*?" she grumbled. "*It's very uncomfortable*."

"*I apologize*," Riasc Tiarna replied. "*I don't spend much time in the company of people. I forget how fragile your kind can be*."

"*I'm not fragile*," Maeve bristled. "*Just tell me what you want*."

"*You aren't long on patience, are you? Your churlishness is insulting and ungrateful, consider-ing I'm here to help you*."

"*Help me how*?" Maeve asked warily.

"*I have come to warn you*."

"*Well, you're too late for that. I have already been betrayed by everyone I know*," Maeve retorted, becoming cross once more at the memory of how the Druids and her family had treated her.

"*Perhaps,*" Riasc Tiarna replied. "*But that is not what I've come to warn you about.*"

"*What else can there be? My life can hardly get worse.*"

"*You have no idea. And that is probably just as well.*"

At the notion that more trouble lay ahead, the bottom fell out of Maeve's stomach. "*What do you mean? What else is going to happen?*"

"*Know that someone—indeed a great many people—are going to need your help. The task will seem impossible, but—*"

Maeve felt him shrug. "*But what?*" She urged the dragon to finish his thought.

"*Know that the task is mightily important and you are the only one who can do it.*"

Maeve stared at the dragon's eyes, trying to determine his sincerity.

"*I don't believe you,*" she announced with finality. "*You're making this up.*"

"*Why would I do that?*"

It was Maeve's turn to shrug. "*How do I know? I've never had dealings with a dragon before. Maybe you are playing a joke on me. Maybe you are trying to scare me.*"

"*Dragons seldom joke,*" Riasc Tiarna said drily. "*And I assure you I am not trying to scare you. I've already done that.*"

It was true. When Maeve had awakened to find a dragon breathing on her, she had almost died of fright.

62

"*As I have already explained, I am trying to prepare you for a matter of grave importance that lies ahead.*"

"*Prove it,*" Maeve sniffed.

The dragon's eyes widened, and a flume of luminous yellow smoke puffed from his nose holes.

"*You're a pushy little thing, aren't you?*"

"*I'm not pushy at all,*" Maeve shot back. "*It's others who push me about. I've simply decided it's time they stopped. Tell me why I should believe this warning you say you bring me. How can you know what will happen?*"

"*The same way you do.*"

"*But I don't. Bradan only says I do.*"

"*The old Druid knows of what he speaks.*"

That the dragon and Bradan might be acquainted caught Maeve by surprise. "*You know Bradan?*"

Ignoring her question, Riasc Tiarna continued. "*Would you heed my warning if I told you that at this precise moment you are struggling with another dilemma—not of the same magnitude as the decision you'll be asked to make in the future, but worrisome nonetheless? You have left the home of your parents. Your sister has turned you away, and you have no other family or friends to help you. The old Druid has asked you to be his apprentice, but he has been dishonest with you, and you are hesitant to accept his offer. Still, you must decide what to do.*"

Maeve caught her breath. *"How do you know all that?"*

"It matters not. Suffice it to say that I do. I would never have mentioned it, except that you demanded proof that I know your future. Since I have done as you asked, will you now heed my warning?"

It was as if Maeve hadn't heard him. *"Can you tell me how I solve my dilemma? Will I go with the Druids? Will my sister change her mind and let me stay with her? Will I crawl to my parents and beg them to take me back?"* She hated the idea of the last option, but she might not have a choice.

"It is not for me to say."

"But you know."

The dragon once again ignored her. *"Will you heed my warning?"*

Maeve heaved an irritated sigh. Though she'd only met Riasc Tiarna this night, she already suspected he would not give in to hounding.

"Fine," she conceded irritably. *"At least tell me what I shall be asked to do. And why I will be asked. Will I be compelled to take on this challenge you speak of? Or can I refuse? If I do attempt it, will I succeed?"*

"You are the one who determines your path— you alone—and always you. I am here only to make you aware that a great decision lies ahead, so that when the time arrives, you will be prepared."

"How can I prepare for something I know nothing about?" Maeve demanded.

"*Have faith. And be brave.*" The dragon stood up. "*Now I must go. I give you leave to stay here for the remainder of the night.*"

To her surprise, Maeve found she didn't want Riasc Tiarna to go.

"*You are perfectly safe here.*" The disappearance of his eyes and the shuddering of the cave told Maeve he was leaving, and though she could see nothing, she stared into the darkness until the cave stopped shaking and she knew Riasc Tiarna was gone.

So when his voice rang out in her head once more, she gasped in surprise. "*We shall meet again, young Maeve,*" it said. Then her mind became quiet.

CHAPTER 9

Maeve didn't think it was possible to fall asleep after all that had happened, but she did. When she awoke again, the cave was as dark as ever, but she felt rested, so she knew it had to be morning.

She sat up and listened. But there were no sounds in the cave—or in her head. She sniffed the air. There was a damp, earthy odour, but no scent of dragon. She waved her arm through the air—no steamy dragon breath to make her sweat either.

She'd thought Riasc Tiarna might still be there, but it seemed he really had gone. His body had gone, that was certain. But Maeve couldn't help feeling he was still with her, listening to her thoughts. That was unnerving. It was one thing to exchange thoughts with a dragon when she chose to, but some thoughts were private, and Maeve didn't fancy sharing those with anyone. Still, it was a comfort to think that Riasc Tiarna was within thinking distance should she need him. It made her feel less alone.

Maeve wondered at how much her life had changed in but a day. Here she was feeling she had a friend in a dragon. Yesterday she would have scoffed at the idea.

She fumbled her way around the wall to the entrance and then up the tunnel. Gradually the blackness turned to grey, becoming ever brighter, until finally she could see where she was going.

As she stepped into the forest, she squinted against the spears of morning sunlight shooting through the trees. She scanned the area for signs of the dragon—flattened ground cover, broken bushes and branches, indentations in the earth— but there was nothing. How could a creature so large leave no evidence of having been there?

Unless he hadn't been, Maeve thought. Perhaps she had dreamt him. Perhaps he was merely a trick of her mind.

She thought of his paralyzing yellow eyes and shivered. No. He had been real—a very real dragon. Maeve knew about such creatures, though she'd never encountered one before. No one she knew had either, so there was no way of telling if the stories she'd heard were true. Some said dragons were giant scaly worms that lurked in fens and bogs. Others claimed they had legs and wings, clawed feet, skin like leather—and they breathed fire. Maeve thought about Riasc Tiarna's steamy breath and decided fire was a definite possibility. Though she hadn't actually seen him, she had no doubt he was huge. The cave had quaked beneath his step. She'd heard stories about dragons terrorizing villages and swallowing hapless residents in one gulp. Yet there were also folk who insisted the creatures were protectors of

67

the land. Since the stories seemed to contradict one another, Maeve wondered if the nature of dragons' deeds depended on the sort of mood they were in. Or perhaps there were simply different kinds of dragons.

If that were so, it would appear that Riasc Tiarna was the good kind. After all, he had sought her out to deliver a warning, though how he should know her future was a mystery. Maeve frowned. Riasc Tiarna's intentions might have been good, but his warning made no sense. He'd said the well-being of many people would rest on her shoulders, and she would be faced with a seemingly impossible task. What did that mean? Maeve heaved a mighty sigh. It seemed dragons—like Druids—had a fondness for riddles.

There was no point worrying about that now, she decided, pushing thoughts of Riasc Tiarna aside. She had other problems—like where she was going to go and what she was going to do. Her stomach growled. And what she was going to eat.

Maeve headed toward the part of the forest she knew well, pondering her options. As much as she felt a oneness with the woods, she couldn't imagine living here on her own. She had no tools or provisions—not even a cup or knife—and in a few months it would be winter. How could she find food or make a shelter? Riasc Tiarna had let her spend the night in his cave, but he probably wouldn't appreciate her living there permanently.

She sighed and thought some more. If the forest wasn't the answer, then perhaps she could earn her keep in the village. Despite her mother's claims, Maeve did know how to work. She might be given only food and a place to sleep in payment for her labour, but that would do until she got herself sorted. Yes, the village was a better option than the forest.

But first she must eat. Spying some blackberry bushes heavy with fruit, Maeve made a bowl of her apron and began filling it. When she had gathered enough fruit to satisfy her hunger, she climbed onto a large fallen log to eat and think.

As she gobbled the juicy berries, she heard a rustling in the bushes behind her. Startled, she jumped down from the log and spun around, flinging berries everywhere. Her heart was pounding so hard in her chest, it hurt.

The bushes continued to move, and Maeve got ready to run. She couldn't think what creature might be pushing through them. Perhaps it was Riasc Tiarna again, but if it wasn't, she needed to get away.

If it was Riasc Tiarna, she wanted to see him, so instead of distancing herself, she ducked behind the log and listened. The rustling got louder. Whatever it was, it was getting closer.

Then everything went quiet. Maeve strained to hear anything that might tell her the intruder's whereabouts, but there was no sound. Slowly and noiselessly she rose to peer over the top of the log.

"I thought I might find you here," Bradan said, smiling down at her.

Maeve was so shocked her knees gave way, and she crumpled to the ground. She could hear the old man chuckling. She scrambled to her feet and scowled at him.

"That's not funny. You scared me! What if I'd had a weapon? If I'd clubbed you with a rock, you wouldn't be laughing, would you?"

"I'm sorry," Bradan apologized, though his eyes twinkled and his lips quivered, and Maeve didn't think he was sorry at all.

"What are you doing here?" Maeve pointed to the forest behind the old man. "The Druid camp is that way."

"I know well where it is, my girl." Bradan sighed. "I've come looking for you."

"Why?" Maeve regarded him warily.

"I said I would return this morning for your answer to my proposal. Have you forgotten? When your parents told me you'd left the cottage last evening and hadn't returned, I suspected I would find you in the forest."

"It's a big forest. Why here? Did you see me in a vision?" She added the last sarcastically.

He ignored the barb. "It is the part of the forest that you know." He nodded toward the blackberry bushes. "And even a runaway needs to eat."

Maeve crossed her arms over her chest and set her jaw stubbornly. Bradan was patronizing her, and she would not be treated like a child. "Well, you've come this way for nothing. I am not going to be your apprentice."

"Ah." He nodded thoughtfully. "You are afraid."

"I am not!" Maeve retorted.

"No?"

"No! You plotted behind my back. I don't trust you now. You and Declan tricked me. He took me to the Druid camp so you could question me, which you did without once explaining what you were doing or why. You didn't give any thought at all to what I might think about the whole thing."

Bradan was clearly taken aback. His mouth dropped open, and he stared unblinking at Maeve for so long she wondered if he had turned to stone.

Finally he said, "I am so sorry, Maeve. You are absolutely right. I have treated you badly indeed. But don't blame Declan. The boy was merely doing my bidding. I didn't want him to say anything about the matter until I had assured myself of your gift. The truth is I didn't want to get your hopes up in case I was wrong. I thought that if you knew I suspected you were a seer, you would be too self-conscious to be yourself. Still, that is a shameful excuse, and I had no right to assume I knew what was best for you. Of course you are upset."

Maeve didn't need Bradan to tell her she had a right to be upset. She knew it full well herself, and she had no trouble giving him a piece of her mind either. Hurt and resentment had been building up inside her her whole life, and it felt good to let it out. It was like she was a flask that had popped its cork.

But she wasn't just angry; she was wounded too. She had opened herself to the Druids, making herself vulnerable, and they had taken advantage. Declan and Bradan had plotted behind her back, and their duplicity had hurt her in a way that couldn't be swept aside with a mere apology.

Maeve lifted her chin higher and sniffed self-righteously. Better to arm herself with anger. It was the least Bradan deserved.

The old man lowered his head so that his beard lay on his chest. He looked truly crestfallen, and though she tried to harden her heart against him, she couldn't quite manage it.

It was obvious Bradan had heard what she'd said. For the first time in her life, someone had listened to her and been affected by her words. It made her feel stronger and more confident. So why was she finding it difficult to stay angry?

Was it possible that Bradan truly had made a mistake but hadn't realized it until Maeve pointed it out? Perhaps—in a way—she was partly to blame for that. She'd assumed the old man was perfect, but he was only human after all. People did make mistakes. Besides, he *had* apologized, and he *did* seem to be honestly sorry.

The old Druid extended his hands. "Please, Maeve. Won't you reconsider?"

She set her jaw again and shook her head.

Bradan closed his eyes and took a deep breath before trying once more to convince her. "I realize now that it was wrong of me to keep the truth from you, and for that I can do nothing but apologize and promise it will never happen again. But I am asking you to look past that and let me help you master your gift. You are one of the most promising seers I have ever met. Do you have any idea how important that is?"

Maeve shook her head again.

"Child, once you learn how to use your sight, there is no end to the good you can do. This land and its people need you. Even kings will come to you for guidance."

"Kings come to *you*," Maeve reminded him. "Why would that change? You are learned and wise. I am anything but that."

"You are young." Bradan smiled. "I shall not live forever. I need someone to take my place. Do not turn your back on your gift, Maeve."

"But I'm not a Druid," Maeve protested. "I don't know anything about Druid ways. I won't fit in." Not that she fit in with her family or the villagers, she thought, but at least she knew what to expect from them.

"You will learn. We will teach you."

"But—" Maeve began and then stopped.

"But what?" Bradan urged her gently. "There is no obstacle that cannot be overcome."

Maeve hesitated. She was afraid of making herself vulnerable again. Finally she blurted,

"What if you're wrong? What if I'm not a seer? What will happen to me then?"

"Oh, child," the old man said softly. "If there is one thing in this world I am certain of, it is your gift and how mighty it is. All it wants is nurturing, and I can see to that. Please—let me teach you. Be my apprentice. If it feels wrong, you needn't stay."

CHAPTER 10

It took much cajoling on Bradan's part, but Maeve eventually agreed to become his apprentice. That didn't mean she forgave him for what he'd done. And she certainly didn't forgive Declan. He had to have known she liked him—how could he not? And he had taken advantage of her feelings to trick her. She was not about to let him fool her again though, no matter how sweet his words. She would keep her distance.

In the beginning it wasn't that difficult. Declan and Finn generally spent their days away from the camp so that Declan would be free of distractions as he learned his stories.

The Druid camp consisted of two shelters where the meadow met the wood—one for the women and the other for the men. The sleeping quarters were simple lean-tos with pine bough walls and roofs. There were no windows. Scraps of rough cloth served as doors. Set among the trees as they were, and made from the forest itself, the shelters were practically invisible unless a body knew to look for them. Enda told Maeve they were built that way not to hide the Druids but out of respect for the forest. They needed shelter, yes, but they had no right to destroy the forest to create it. The cottage Maeve had grown up in was far from grand, but compared to the Druid shelters, it was a castle.

Bradan told Maeve the camp was a temporary base—a place where masters could work with their apprentices in the solitude of nature. Not that everyone in camp was an apprentice or teacher. For the most part, Ohdran, Enda and Cara saw to practical matters such as wood chopping, cooking, healing and bartering with the farmers and village folk for the items they needed. In a few months, though, they would all leave this place and gather with Druids from across the land to celebrate winter solstice. Then they would return to their homes and families until the warmer weather returned and it was time to venture out with their apprentices once more.

Within a week of joining the Druid camp, Maeve was already questioning her decision. Despite Bradan's conviction that she was a seer, she saw no signs of it. Perhaps she had expected something miraculous to happen to validate his belief in her, but no such thing occurred. If anything, she was tripping over herself more than ever.

To make matters worse, she didn't understand Druid ways, so getting through a day without misstepping was a challenge. Druids were much more complicated than she had realized. Even the colours of their robes had meaning. Elders wore white, but bards wore blue, while most everyone else wore brown. Bradan said the robe of the Arch-Druid was gold! As far as she could tell, the Druids were a people of contradictions. They were humble in their dealings with nature but held great power over common folk. They were simultaneously respected and feared.

Maeve's apprenticeship should have been a wonderful awakening, but it wasn't. Despite Bradan's assurances, all she felt was frustration and fear that she would never fit into Druid life, and that she wasn't a seer, just a dreamer. Bradan had said she could leave if she didn't feel comfortable, and she was considering it.

"It shouldn't be this hard!" she moaned to Enda as they prepared for bed. "If I am really a seer, shouldn't I have some sense of it?"

Enda shrugged. "I can't say. All I know is that it takes a very long time to become adept at any calling, no matter how gifted a person is. You can't expect results overnight. That's why we apprentice years with our masters."

"But I feel like a fraud. How can I be a seer if I'm not a Druid?"

Enda shrugged again. "Don't fret so. Druids and common folk are not so different. We all need to eat and sleep. We are the same creatures. It is only in our teachings that we are different."

"But Druids are born Druids and the rest of us are not," said Maeve.

Enda smiled kindly. "I know not why you have come to us. I do know that Bradan is wise. If he says you are a seer, then you are."

So Maeve stayed.

———

"It is a balance," Bradan told Maeve as they walked through the forest one morning.

She sighed. "That is your answer to everything."

"Because it is so. One need only observe nature to see the truth of it." The old Druid shrugged. "We must always strive for balance."

Maeve cocked her head and regarded Bradan through narrowed eyes. "Must I learn to speak in riddles like you if I am to become a seer?"

The old man threw back his head and guffawed mightily.

Maeve frowned. "Why are you laughing?"

When Bradan's chuckles subsided, he said, "I'm not laughing at you, child. I am merely enjoying your honesty. The world will steal that from you soon enough. Take joy in it while you can."

But Maeve barely heard. Her mind had already jumped to her next thought. "Bradan, how do you know the meaning of the things you see in your head, and how can you be certain your interpretations are right? How can you know the meaning of the visions and dreams of others? And—"

The Druid chuckled again. "Goodness, child. If it took only a breath or two to give you answers, you wouldn't need a teacher. Being a seer has more to do with feeling and less to do with knowing. Once you learn to open yourself to your feelings and trust in what they tell you, you will have the answers you seek."

Maeve frowned and muttered, "More riddles."

Bradan smiled and patted her shoulder. "Patience, child. That is the first lesson."

He stopped at a tall pine tree and ran his hand over the bark of the trunk. Then he leaned in and inhaled its earthy smell.

Maeve watched him. "Why are you doing that?"

The old man ignored her question. "Isn't nature wondrous?" He spread his arms to take in the forest surrounding them before bending down to pick up a pine cone. He gestured to the tree again. "This giant began as a tiny seed inside a cone such as this and survived despite all odds."

He held the cone high in the air and turned it one way and then the other, as if it were a gemstone sparkling in the sun. Then he ran his hand over the cone's rough scales and beckoned Maeve to come closer.

"You see all these petals?"

Maeve nodded.

"At the base of each are the seeds."

"I thought the cone was the seed."

Bradan shook his head. "The cone merely houses the seeds and protects them until it is time for them to be freed. There are two seeds at the base of each petal." He shrugged. "Well, not in this particular cone. As you can see, the petals of this cone are open, which means the seeds have already been sent into the world."

He stooped to the ground and retrieved a second cone. It was green and its petals were tightly closed. "This one is still protecting its seeds, and since it has already fallen, it will likely never release them. Not all cones do."

He dropped the unripe cone and turned his attention back to the first one. "Of the many seeds that were within this cone, perhaps only one will take root. If many seeds take root, perhaps only one will grow. Perhaps none of them will." He pointed to the multitude of cones beneath the tree. "But there are so many cones and so many chances. Some will be successful."

Maeve supposed Bradan was right. Being a farmer's daughter, she knew well enough that plants grew from seeds, but she'd never thought of it as amazing—she'd never thought about it at all. It was merely something that was.

"Why don't they all grow?" she asked.

"Why are you asking me? You know the answer yourself."

"I do?"

"How many trees do you see here?"

Maeve looked around her. "Lots."

"And if all the seeds grew?"

In her mind Maeve saw the roots tangling beneath the soil and the branches jostling one another as they competed for sunlight. She saw trees stunted and dying for want of water, so that instead of growing, the forest was shrinking.

"There would be too many," she said.

"So why don't they all grow?" Bradan turned her question back on her.

Maeve rolled her eyes and sighed. "Balance."

"Indeed."

———

Bradan had said patience was the first lesson Maeve must learn, but he neglected to tell her she would be required to complete many tasks in order to learn it.

"Is it full yet?" Enda asked.

"No," Maeve grumbled from the tree stump where she sat huddled in her mantle, watching raindrops fall into an iron pot. "Not even half. Bradan said I must sit here and watch until it is brimming. I could be here forever!"

Enda glanced skyward. "Not much fear of that, I'd say. It's raining fairly hard, and it looks to me as if it's going to be like that all day."

"Why is Bradan making me collect water one pot at a time anyway?" Maeve groused. "The rain barrel at the edge of the meadow is already full. And why must I sit here and watch every single drop? I could be doing something much more useful."

Enda shrugged. "Why don't you ask him?"

"I did."

"And his answer?"

Maeve sighed and did her best Bradan impersonation. "Patience, child." Then she growled through her teeth.

Enda laughed. "Well then, I'll leave you to it."

It was the longest day of Maeve's life. She

couldn't think of a more useless waste of time. When it was over, all she felt was damp, cold, restless and grumpy—about as far from patient as a body could be.

To her dismay, Bradan had an equally tedious task for her the next day. This time he gave her over to a farmer's wife who set her down with several baskets of raw sheep's wool from which she was to pick burrs, twigs and grass spears. By the time she returned to the Druid camp that evening, her fingers were cramped and sore, and she could barely see straight.

And so it went. Day after day, Bradan set challenges for her that made the hours drag. She had to watch a spider spin its web, pull the scales from a pine cone to examine its core, stand perfectly still in the forest until a woodland creature came close enough to touch, and, worst of all, endure an entire day without speaking.

Thoughts and questions she was not permitted to voice bubbled up inside her until Maeve was sure she would burst. But as the day wore on she realized it wasn't so bad being quiet. In some ways it was pleasant. Wandering about the meadow and through the woodland, she found herself noticing every sound and seeing things she would otherwise have walked past. As she tended to her chores, the conversations she would normally have been a part of seemed somehow different. Instead of listening to make a reply, Maeve found herself listening to understand.

At the start of the day she had been a tightly capped flask of energy and frustration, but when she took to her bed that night, her mind and body settled in a way they never had before—like two rivers becoming one. She was at peace.

CHAPTER 11

Maeve was usually too busy to notice if Declan was in the camp. Her days and mind were full to overflowing with training to be a seer and learning the Druid ways. When she fell onto the rude bed she shared with Enda each night, she was too tired to think of anything—or anyone. All she wanted was to sleep.

But, of course, that couldn't continue forever. As the days settled into a routine, Maeve sometimes found herself at the water barrel at the same time as Declan or collecting wood as he was chopping it. When their paths crossed, Maeve would jump out of the way as if he were a wild animal to be avoided. None of their encounters lasted more than a moment, but even so, Maeve would mumble hello while avoiding eye contact and hurry on her way.

So when Bradan announced that the mistress of a nearby farm had invited the Druids to collect the windfall from the autumn crop of apples, and that Maeve and Declan were to gather the fruit, she was more than a little anxious. She was being thrown together with him, and there was nothing she could do about it.

After a stiff greeting on the morning of their task, they walked the distance to the farm in silence. Maeve's head was filled with imagined conversation, but her lips were sealed shut. If Declan had any inkling of her discomfort, he did not show it. All she knew was that he seemed in a great hurry, and she had to run to keep up with him.

There were a lot of apples, and the two young people quickly filled the sacks they had brought. Then, without a word, Declan started back to the camp and Maeve followed.

But it was one thing to drag the sack around the orchard as she filled it with apples and quite another to haul it to the Druid camp. It wasn't long before she was huffing and puffing and had to stop.

"Do you need help?" Declan called to her.

His question caused her back to stiffen with stubbornness.

"No," she snapped. She dug deep within herself for strength and resumed dragging the sack. "I'm fine."

Declan looked ready to argue, but then he shrugged and continued moving forward.

Maeve suspected he slowed his pace to allow for her struggle with the sack, but he never asked again if she needed help. When they eventually reached the Druid camp, they left their sacks of apples with Cara and—to Maeve's relief—went their separate ways.

———

Maeve wandered through the forest with her basket over her arm and her gaze fixed on the ground. A few steps away, Enda did the same. They were searching for mushrooms. As they poked around the trees, Maeve stepped carefully. Mushrooms liked to hide under fallen leaves, and she had no desire to stomp on her dinner.

This was her first time foraging for mushrooms. Stories of folk eating the wrong ones, becoming ill and dying had convinced Maeve's mother that mushrooms were too dangerous, so until Maeve came to the Druids, she had never tasted one. But it was mushroom season, which meant they were a regular part of Druid meals. No one in camp had become sick from eating them, and Maeve had no desire to go hungry, so she had set aside her misgivings and tried them. To her great relief, she hadn't died—or even become ill. And when cooked with wild garlic, mushrooms were quite tasty. At first she'd found the texture strange, but the flavour quickly won her over, and after a while she didn't notice the feel of them anymore.

"And these?" Maeve called to Enda as she pushed the leaves away from a brown cluster near the base of a tree. "Are these ones safe to eat?"

Enda picked her way through the undergrowth to Maeve. She freed one of the mushrooms from the soil, turned it over and ran her finger along the ridges on the underside. "Yes—brown wavy inside-out hat, ridges and a long, yellow stem. This kind is very tasty." She smiled. "Well done."

Then Enda returned to her own hunt, and Maeve went back to hers. She was so focused on looking for mushrooms that the vision which rushed into her head sent her staggering.

She grabbed onto a tree to steady herself and blinked the world back into focus. Never before had she been struck by a vision in such a way. As the shock subsided, she tried to make sense of what she'd experienced. It was as if she'd been hit between the eyes with a rock. Her head spun with brilliant red and ominous black, swirling and tangling until there was no telling one colour from the other. When the hues were finally so twisted they were indistinguishable, they burst into orange flame and vanished.

Maeve shook her head. It made no sense. She doubted even Bradan would have known what to make of it.

Though she was curious to have her vision explained, Maeve decided to keep it to herself. Her mind played host to so many strange things, it was impossible to tell which ones meant something and which were merely the result of a wild imagination. She couldn't trouble Bradan with every one. She would wait. If she had the vision again, she would say something.

Every night after the evening meal, the Druids gathered round a bonfire to listen to Master Finn tell stories. It was a ritual Maeve looked forward to with great anticipation. Finn was considered the best bard in the land, and it was easy to see why. He had a way about him that was mesmerizing. It didn't matter what tale he told, Maeve was always spellbound. He spoke softly, but the timbre of his voice drew her in, and she was helpless to resist the deep, resonant tones that filled the darkness.

This night, though, it was not Finn who was to regale them with a tale, but Declan.

As a bard's apprentice, it made sense that he would practise his skills on listeners other than Finn. And even if he was no longer her friend, Maeve was curious to hear him tell a story.

She took her usual place at the fire beside Enda. The crackling blaze stood between her and Declan, washing him with a yellow glow. If he was nervous, he showed no sign.

"Long, long ago, the first people to this land came from beyond the eastern sea," he began quietly. Though Maeve could hear him well enough, she found herself leaning forward. "They were fleeing oppression, and when their boats slid onto the beach, they stepped ashore with little more than their lives. But they had hope, and with that they set forth to explore the lush green hills and forests.

"Finding the land teeming with promise, they built homes and planted crops, and were well pleased to have found freedom at last. Theirs was a hard existence, but they were in harmony with nature and each other, and their troubles were few. Life was simple but good, and thus it remained for many years."

As Declan described that long-ago time, Maeve became one with those early settlers. Alongside them she heard the morning song of the birds, smelled the freshly turned earth and felt the sun on her face. When dusk gave way to darkness, she heard the frogs croak and the crickets chirp, while the weariness of hard work settled into her bones and contentment soothed her soul.

"Over time more boats found the island, and the population grew and prospered, settling in pockets near this stream or that meadow, and villages naturally grew.

"But this idyllic existence was not to last." Declan's voice took on a hard edge, jerking Maeve from her reverie. "Disaster arrived beneath a storm-grey sky, crashing onto the shore in great ships from the north. Like a raucous black wave, the invaders rolled southward over the land, swinging axes and leaving a swath of destruction in their wake. One after the other, villages were razed, and the earth became soaked with blood. Thick smoke turned day to night, and those who managed to elude their attackers took to the forest, crazed with terror. They huddled in hollow logs and thorny bushes, imagining their deaths, for they were certain there was no escape.

"And they were right.

"From nowhere, a giant winged creature with razor-sharp claws and shimmering black scales appeared above them. They watched the sky turn to fire. Angry orange tongues of flame licked the treetops and set them snapping and crackling like kindling. Trapped below, the villagers stared in horror as the blaze jumped from branch to branch and slid down the tree trunks. There was nowhere to hide, and soon not even the dense black smoke could swallow the villagers' anguished screams. Only death could do that."

Every muscle in Maeve's body had become taut. As sure as she was sitting beside Enda at this very moment, she had huddled with those people trapped in the forest. She had been with those who were struck down in the villages too. Listening to Declan, she died a thousand deaths.

"A red dragon inhabited the island too—this place had been his home long before the arrival of people. The din of the attack awakened him in his lair. Sniffing fire and blood, he thundered from his cave. Someone—or something—was wreaking havoc in his land. His yellow eyes narrowed as he beheld the devastation. Then he glanced skyward and spied a black dragon gliding over the forest. He took to the air, his strong wings swiftly cutting the distance between them. The black dragon was no stranger. The red dragon knew him well—and despised him more. Wherever he went, he brought death and destruction. And now it

90

appeared he and his army of thieves and murderers had set their sights on the red dragon's land.

"The black dragon sensed his enemy before he saw him and swung around to confront him, only to be hit full in the face with a stream of molten fire. Angered more than injured, he let loose his own fire, but the red dragon had already shifted position, and the flame shot harmlessly past him. The two danced in the air, lunging and spinning, twisting and dodging, snarling and snapping. With claws extended and fangs bared, they came together and pulled away again and again, hurling fire while their tails swayed menacingly from side to side, waiting for the chance to strike.

"The sparring continued for some time, faster and faster, until the two were so entwined they had become a single whorl of red and black. Finally there was a shriek so sharp it froze the hearts of every living creature within earshot.

"The war in the sky was over and the combatants pulled away—one roaring victoriously and spewing fire, and the other whimpering in defeat. Then without so much as a final snarl, the black dragon limped across the sky from whence he had come."

Maeve felt the tension that had been building inside her melt away, and she released the breath she hadn't realized she'd been holding. She glanced around the fire. The others looked relieved too. Then a cheer went up, and Declan smiled shyly.

The Druids got to their feet and one by one congratulated the young man on the fine telling of his story. Maeve went last.

"That was very exciting, Declan," she said, pushing past the awkwardness that now marked their relationship. "Your story made me shiver. I felt like it was happening to me."

He grinned. "Thank you, Maeve. That means a lot."

"Could I ask you one thing?"

"Of course."

"Did the dragons have names?"

Declan grimaced and slapped his forehead with the heel of his hand. "I knew I'd forgotten something." He sighed. "Yes, they had names. Because of the grief he caused, the people called the black dragon Misery."

"And the red one?"

"That was Riasc Tiarna, Lord of the Marshes."

CHAPTER 12

Maeve spent a restless night tossing and turning and fending off irritated jabs from Enda. When she had joined the Druids, she'd set aside the memory of the dragon she met in the cave. But thanks to Declan it was once again foremost in her thoughts, and though his story provided answers to some of her questions, it also gave rise to new mysteries.

She now understood the vision she'd had while picking mushrooms. The swirls of red and black that had burst into her mind represented the battle between the dragons. What she didn't understand was why she'd been shown that. As a seer, she was supposed to have insights into the future, but that vision reflected an event from the past. Certainly, she hadn't known about the battle, and the vision foreshadowed the story Declan told around the fire, but the battle itself was old news.

Maeve yawned and pushed her breakfast around in her bowl. If she had learned anything from Bradan, it was that there was always a reason for visions. So what was the reason for this one?

She took a mouthful of porridge and thought some more.

One of the dragons in Declan's tale had been called Riasc Tiarna, Lord of the Marshes. That was the name of the dragon Maeve had met in the cave. Was it the same creature? She didn't see how it could be. Declan's dragon had lived hundreds of years ago, and Maeve met hers only a few months ago. Could her Riasc Tiarna be a descendant of that long-ago dragon?

She closed her eyes and shook her head. It was all too confusing.

"You'd best eat up." Enda's voice broke into Maeve's thoughts. "Bradan is waiting for you."

Maeve quickly shovelled the rest of her porridge into her mouth. She'd completely forgotten she was to accompany Bradan to the village. Every few weeks he went there to mingle with the townsfolk and interpret their dreams, but this was the first time he'd invited her to go along.

She hadn't been to the village since the last time she'd sold eggs for her mother. She was very much looking forward to the outing, especially since it was a sign she was moving forward in her training. Even so, she was apprehensive. Bradan had said all she need do was observe, but Maeve knew he would have many questions for her afterward, and she feared she would not have the answers.

As was her habit, Maeve gave herself up to the forest as they made their way along the trail. The leaves on the ground, which only yesterday had crunched beneath her feet, were limp and silent.

She turned her face to the sun, but there was no warmth in its rays. It saddened her to think that autumn was spent, and the winter rains would soon be upon them.

"That was a fine story Declan told last night," she said to distract herself.

"Indeed it was," Bradan agreed, using his stick to push aside the vines and branches in their path.

"Was it true?"

The old man paused mid-stride and regarded her curiously. "Declan's story?"

Maeve nodded. "Yes. Did it really happen?"

Bradan raised an eyebrow. "What a strange thing to ask. Bards aren't in the habit of making tales up. The whole point is to recount events so they aren't lost or forgotten."

"Then there really *are* dragons?" Maeve blurted, immediately regretting her impulsiveness. The tone of her voice suggested she had more than a casual reason for asking, and the last thing she wanted was to arouse Bradan's curiosity. He'd start asking his own questions, and like as not she'd end up telling him about the dragon in the cave. Since she didn't wish to talk about that, she hurried on before he could reply. "Have you ever seen one?"

"Once," he replied, "but that was a very long time ago."

"Really?" Maeve was genuinely surprised. Though Riasc Tiarna hadn't admitted he knew Bradan, perhaps he did. Forgetting her resolve to steer the conversation elsewhere, she asked,

"What dragon was it? Where did you see it? Was it fierce or friendly?"

Bradan sighed. "Always so many questions. I can see you haven't yet acquired the virtue of patience. Perhaps you are in need of more lessons."

Inside, Maeve quailed. Another lesson in patience was the last thing she needed—well, it was the last thing she *wanted* at any rate. She bit back the other questions threatening to trip off her tongue and said instead, "I think Declan is going to make a fine bard."

"Indeed," the old man gruffly replied.

———

When they arrived in the village, the square was already a hive of activity. Maeve followed behind Bradan as he walked among the villagers discussing the weather, the year's fine harvest and whether or not the country might soon be at war. He bought a few items too—salt, flour and a slab of pork fat. The supplies would certainly be welcomed by Cara, who did most of the Druids' cooking, but the real reason for the purchases was to ensure he was noticed, so that the villagers could spread the word to anyone needing his counsel—which, of course, they did. Maeve observed this quietly, all the while staying in Bradan's shadow. Even so, more than once she found herself being eyed curiously by the villagers. No doubt they had heard she'd joined the Druids and were trying to figure out what Bradan saw in her that they didn't.

Word of Bradan's presence spread, and by mid-morning the old Druid couldn't move for the crowd of people around him—some hoping to have their dreams explained but most simply wanting to eavesdrop on their neighbours' affairs.

Before Maeve came to live among the Druids, she'd been unaware of just how much impact they had on the lives of common folk. They might not live among them, but they made themselves a presence—as Bradan was doing this morning. The kings and chieftains ruled the land, but it was the Druids who provided moral and spiritual leadership.

As Maeve watched Bradan converse with the villagers, she was reminded of the first time she'd met him and how his unfeigned warmth had put her at ease. People were naturally drawn to him. But he had an air of authority about him too, and he prompted such trust Maeve was sure he could lead people over the edge of a cliff if he'd a mind to. When he interpreted their dreams, they hung on his every word.

"You're sure?" A man cocked an eyebrow and regarded Bradan skeptically. "Me future son-in-law ain't plotting against me? I'll not be murdered in me bed?"

Bradan solemnly shook his head. "You have nothing to fear on that account, I assure you."

"So why'd I dream it then?"

Bradan shrugged. "Your dream is a parable of sorts. It isn't so much a sign of what is going to happen as it is a reflection of how you're feeling about what is going on right now. You are a widower, are you not?"

The man nodded.

"And you have but one child—a daughter, who is about to marry. Is that correct?"

The man nodded again.

"It all makes perfect sense then."

"What does?"

"Well, even though you haven't said so, your dream indicates that you will miss your daughter when she is wed and that you feel like she is being stolen from you. Since everyone else is happy about the marriage, you feel as if they are plotting against you."

The man frowned. "I *will* miss her. That is true enough. With me wife gone, I'll be all on me own." He squinted at the old Druid. "You think that's it then?"

It was Bradan's turn to nod.

"But what about being killed in me bed?" the man demanded. "How d'ya explain that bit?"

Bradan looked around at the expectant faces in the crowd, then beckoned the man to come nearer. When he did, Bradan whispered in his ear.

After a few seconds the man pulled away, obviously surprised. "You don't say? Really?"

"Yes."

The fellow grinned. "Well, I'll be jiggered. Ain't that somethin'! Thank ye, Druid."

He dug into his breeches for a coin and pushed

it into Bradan's hand. "Thank ye greatly. I'm much obliged."

As the man loped off, a hum of speculation arose among the curious bystanders. What had Bradan said to the man?

The Druid cleared his throat. "Does anyone else need a dream explained?"

A young woman partway round the circle from Maeve stepped forward. "Yes, seer, I do."

Maeve caught her breath. It was Deirdre. Maeve hadn't noticed her, and Deirdre must not have seen Maeve either. She would never have spoken up if she had, and she would certainly withdraw if she realized Maeve was there. Deirdre generally kept her own counsel. Something must be troubling her greatly if she was seeking Bradan's advice. Even without knowing what it was, Maeve wanted to rush forward, hug her sister and tell her everything would be fine. But she knew that would only chase her away. Instead, she slipped behind a large man and let a woman with a small child slide into her place.

"Tell me your dream," Bradan said.

There was silence, and Maeve peeked around the man. Deirdre was frowning, clearly trying to decide whether to speak up or turn around and go home.

"Take your time," Bradan urged her gently.

More silence, and the man in front of Maeve muttered, "Get on with it."

Maeve gave him a push, and when he whirled

angrily around, she mumbled, "Sorry. I lost my balance."

The man would probably have pursued the matter further, but Deirdre started to speak, so he turned his attention back to the centre of the circle.

"It's a dream I've had many times. I think it's an omen about the child I'm carrying."

Maeve imagined her sister holding her belly.

"Don't assume anything, my dear," Bradan said kindly. "Just tell me your dream."

Deirdre nodded. "It's not a very long dream, but it always wakens me. I know something dreadful is going to happen. In my dream, I'm staring down at my baby in its cradle. I don't know if it's a boy or girl, but my heart is full and I am joyful. Then, for no reason, my happiness leaves me, and as I look at my baby, I start to weep. Soon I'm crying so hard I can't stop, and I feel like my heart is going to break."

"What happens after that?" Bradan asked.

"Nothing. That's when I wake up. What does it mean, seer? Why do I keep having this dream? Am I going to lose my child?"

Maeve could hear the fear in Deirdre's voice, and it was all she could do not to push through the crowd and go to her.

"Don't upset yourself," Bradan said. "It is good that you came to me. You are not going to lose your baby."

"Are you certain?" Deirdre demanded anxiously.

"Absolutely. You are young and healthy. There is no reason to think anything will go awry." He paused. "Your dream does indicate some sort of trouble ahead—trouble concerning a loved one. You transferred that fear to your baby, because babes are helpless and that is how you will feel when this trouble shows itself."

"What—what sort of trouble?" Deirdre stammered. "Will I get past it?"

"We always get past our troubles," Bradan replied. "Not always unscathed, but we carry on. More than that I cannot say."

CHAPTER 13

"So what did you learn about dreams?" Bradan asked as he and Maeve made their way back to the Druid camp.

"That they're never about what they're about," Maeve replied flatly.

Bradan raised an eyebrow. "How so?"

"Think about the young woman in the village. In her dream she was looking at her baby in its cradle and—"

"Your sister, you mean."

Maeve eyed Bradan. She hadn't told him about Deirdre. "How do you know she's my sister?"

He shrugged. "You are of an age to be sisters. Also, you disappeared into the crowd when she stepped forward. I assumed you didn't want her to see you, which would indicate you know each other." He waved the subject away. "It doesn't matter. Go on with what you were saying. I shouldn't have interrupted."

Maeve frowned. Sometimes it irked her that Bradan seemed to know everything. It gave a person no privacy. "Well, as I was saying," she grumbled, "her dream was about the baby, but according to you, it wasn't about the baby at all."

"Mmm," Bradan murmured thoughtfully as he nodded. "I can see how that might be confusing, but once you understand the symbols in dreams, you—"

"Symbols?"

"Things that stand for other things. For instance, a crown often stands for royalty. In your sister's dream, the baby was a symbol for helplessness."

Maeve clucked her tongue. "How do you know that? Does a baby always stand for helplessness?"

"No. Sometimes a baby is simply a baby, and sometimes something else will symbolize helplessness. Every situation is different."

Though she was trying her hardest to follow Bradan's logic, Maeve was lost. "So how do you know when something is really what it is and when it's a symbol for something else? Are you just guessing?"

Bradan didn't reply. Maeve knew he'd heard her, and she was tempted to press him for an answer. But she was afraid he might send more patience lessons her way, so she kept quiet.

Finally he said, "Do you remember me telling you that being a seer had as much to do with feeling as knowing?"

Maeve hesitated. Bradan was forever talking in riddles and presenting her with puzzles. How could she be expected to remember every one? Balance. Patience. Sensing. Feeling. So many things that weren't things at all. Things she couldn't catch hold of, no matter how hard she tried.

"I'm not sure," she confessed.

"It is the balance between the heart and the head," he went on patiently. "With time, you will learn to open your senses, notice everything there is to notice and then weigh those observations in your mind. On the one side you will place what your senses tell you and what your brain knows, and on the other you will set down what your heart and instincts tell you. When you find the balance between the two sides, you will have the truth."

"How will I know when I have the truth?" she asked.

"Do you remember when I asked you to walk through the forest in your mind?"

"Yes."

"When you did that, you were accessing the part of you that walks in the balance."

Maeve still thought it sounded like guessing, but she nodded and kept walking. It was impossible to stop herself from thinking though. After a few moments she forgot her resolve to stay quiet and blurted, "Are you certain Deirdre's baby is all right?"

"As I told your sister, she is young and healthy, so there is no reason to assume there will be a problem."

Then you don't know for sure, Maeve wanted to say, but she bit back the words and asked, "Do you always tell people everything you know about their dreams and visions?"

Again Bradan took his time answering. Finally he replied, "That is an insightful question. It tells me that you are beginning to understand. And it shows me that your lessons in patience have done their job."

It didn't escape Maeve's notice that he hadn't answered her question, but considering his comment about patience, she couldn't very well ask it again. Instead she said, "Are you ever wrong?"

Bradan cocked an eyebrow.

"Have you ever misinterpreted a dream? Misread a situation? Given the wrong advice?"

"More times than I care to remember," he replied. "I'm just a man."

Maeve was surprised. Bradan was the smartest, wisest person she'd ever met. "But you always seem so certain about everything."

"I trust my heart and head to work together and show me the truth, but there are times when I'm fooled." He smiled. "Mistakes keep us humble— as long as we don't make too many."

For a while they walked in silence, and Maeve gave herself up to the spicy scent of pine needles, the clouds scudding past overhead and the treetops dancing with the breeze. It was so calm and restful—she would happily have stayed in the moment forever. When Bradan started talking again, it took a few seconds to focus on what he was saying.

"I have an idea," he said. "We shall give you a dream to interpret."

"What dream?"

"Mine."

Maeve was dubious. It was a lot of pressure to make sense of her teacher's dream, especially since he would already know its meaning. The only thing this exercise was likely to accomplish was to make her look a fool.

He stopped walking, so she did too.

"I want you to relax," he said. "You must let the meaning of the dream come to you. You can't force it. The first step is observation. In this case, you will listen and picture in your mind what I tell you. Then you will think of what you know of me and how the dream might fit into my life. Remember that some of the parts will be symbols for other things. Finally, look into yourself and weigh your thoughts and observations against your instincts."

Maeve took a deep breath and let it out again.

"Do you understand?"

"I think so." She opened her mind as wide as it would go and waited for Bradan to continue.

"Good," Bradan said. "I have had this particular dream only once. In the dream, I am tired, and I am in an unfamiliar place—countryside I don't know. There is someone with me, though I never see the other person's face. After a time we find ourselves surrounded by castles on every side. One is grander than the others, so we make our way there. We are escorted to a great room filled with banners of every colour, shape and size. They are talking banners. No—shouting banners.

The banners are shouting, and they are so loud, I can't hear myself think."

"Then what?" Maeve asked when he stopped speaking.

The old Druid shrugged. "There is no more."

"Oh." Maeve was surprised by the brevity of the dream.

"Don't rush to give me an answer," Bradan said. "This is your first attempt at interpreting a dream. Take your time. Look carefully at all the parts. Turn them round and round until they slide together."

Maeve had no idea what to make of Bradan's dream. Yet somehow she must find a way to untangle it. She tried to recall the things he'd said to focus on—listening, thinking, feeling.

He'd said he was in an unfamiliar land. As far as Maeve knew, he hadn't travelled any-where recently.

"When did you have this dream?" she asked.

"Yesterday."

Perhaps that meant he was going on a journey in the future. Soon, probably, if he was dream-ing about it. *Of course!* The winter solstice was coming up, and Bradan would have to travel a distance for that. Druids from all across the land would gather to celebrate. Perhaps the castles in Bradan's dream symbolized the kingdoms the Druids came from. And perhaps he couldn't identify the fellow traveller in his dream because it was a stranger. It made sense.

So far the puzzle was coming together nicely.

The only part that still needed sorting was the bit about the banners. The banners had to be symbols, because there was no such thing as *talking* banners. Symbols for what, though? Bradan had said symbols could change. Perhaps the banners and castles were both symbols for the Druids, and the reason the banners were shouting was because the winter solstice was a celebration, and celebrations were noisy affairs.

Maeve's whole body had grown tight as she'd worked at unraveling the dream, but now that it was done, she felt her tension drain away. Pleased with her accomplishment, she shared it with Bradan. When he didn't immediately react, her sense of well-being slithered away.

"I got it wrong, didn't I?" she said.

"For a first attempt, you've done well," Bradan countered.

"Not if I got it wrong."

"Your observations were good, as was your logic," the old man said, "but you were forcing things—trying to make them fit. I could see you were as tight as boots two sizes too small. You need to open yourself so understanding flows through you easily and naturally. And you must listen to your inner self, that part of you that instinctively senses when something is right—or isn't."

Though Maeve hated to admit it, Bradan was right. She'd been so happy to have solved the dream, she hadn't taken the time to ask herself if she really believed her interpretation.

For the hundredth time since she'd begun her apprenticeship, Maeve despaired at her stupidity. She kept making the same mistakes over and over. Mastering her gift—if indeed she had a gift—was too difficult. She couldn't complete even the simplest of tasks. And she asked too many questions. All she was trying to do was understand, but Bradan wanted her to figure things out for herself. Didn't he see that she couldn't? Maeve was so discouraged she wanted to run away and hide in Riasc Tiarna's cave forever.

Bradan patted her hand. "Never mind. It takes practice to master these skills. All things considered, I am pleased with your effort."

"What is the real meaning of the dream?" Maeve grumbled. Though she knew the truth would rankle, she still needed to know.

"I am going on a journey," Bradan said. "That part you got right. But the dream wasn't foretelling the winter solstice. In truth, I am being called to a gathering of the kings and chieftains at the bidding of King Redmond. The banners represent everyone at the gathering, and they are shouting because it is a council of war."

Startled out of her sour mood, Maeve gasped. "Are the kingdoms going to war again?"

"Not against each other, no. This time there is a greater enemy—the Norsemen from across the sea."

Maeve's eyes opened as wide as they could

go. "Like the ones in Declan's tale?"

Bradan nodded. "History has a way of repeating itself."

"Is war a certainty?"

"I won't know until after the council meets, but it looks likely."

"And you are going to the council?"

"I must. The king has commanded my presence. And you will accompany me. You are the unidentified traveller in my dream."

Maeve's mouth dropped open. "I am?"

Bradan chuckled. "I have a confession. There was no dream. I made it up to test you. I learned of the council meeting from the king's messenger. He presented himself at our camp yesterday, while you and Enda were picking mushrooms."

Maeve stamped her foot. "You tricked me!" But she wasn't really cross. She was too excited for that. "Are you truly taking me with you?" she said.

"We leave in the morning."

CHAPTER 14

It was barely dawn when Maeve and Bradan set out for the war council. The dregs of night still clung to the trees, and a swirling mist hovered above the ground. Maeve felt as if she was wading into the sea instead of tramping through the forest. She'd come this way many times before, but this morning the path felt untravelled and strange. She supposed it was because of the early hour and the thrill of beginning an adventure.

She scolded herself. This wasn't an adventure. It wasn't a game. The journey was of grave importance. The entire land and all its people might soon be embroiled in a war so devastating she couldn't begin to imagine it.

And that was strange. She thought that as a seer she would know what was coming. She should have had a vision or a dream, but she hadn't. Bradan hadn't either. Perhaps that meant there was nothing to fear. But if that were the case, King Redmond wouldn't have called for a council of war, and Bradan wouldn't be hurrying to attend it.

King Redmond ruled the entire realm, which was made up of nine regions. His castle was in the northernmost kingdom, and the other regions were ruled by lesser kings. These kingdoms were

further divided into territories, which were gov-
erned by clan chieftains. The attendance of every
king and chieftain was required at the council of
war. It would have been held at King Redmond's
castle, but because time was of the essence it
was decided Castle Carrick was a better choice.
It was centrally located in Meath, the home of
King Redmond's brother-in-law, Owen, who was
regarded by many as second in power only to the
Great King himself.

Castle Carrick stood atop a rocky hill, the
perfect fortress, but an exhausting climb for visitors. It was particularly hard on Bradan. Seeing
him wheeze and gasp as he struggled up the steep
slope, it occurred to Maeve—in a way it never had
before—that Bradan was an old man. Suddenly
it wasn't his strong mind and wise words she
was focused on, but his stooped shoulders and
unsteady gait. In the short time she had been with
the Druids, Bradan had become very dear to her.
He was more than her teacher. He was her friend.
He made her feel safe and valued. She could rely
on him for anything, and it troubled her to think he
wouldn't always be there.

Bradan and Maeve arrived at the castle as the
sun was setting on the third day. The council of
war was to commence the next morning.

As they stood before the stone walls waiting
for the portcullis to be raised and the massive
wooden doors to be opened, Bradan said quietly,
"Tomorrow I shall be busy with the council, so I

won't be able to observe everything that is going on. I shall need you to be my eyes and ears. You must be a fly on the wall, seeing and hearing everything without being noticed yourself."

"What should I be looking for?"

"Anything. Everything. Trust your instincts. You will know."

———

As Maeve and Braden were led into the castle, Maeve shivered with excitement. She'd never been close to a castle before, let alone inside one. *And the castle she was in belonged to a king!* She pinched herself to make sure she wasn't dreaming. Everything was so grand. The cavernous rooms were adorned with tapestries and ornate furnishings. There were endlessly long tables, carved chairs, torches and candles, pewter dishes and goblets encrusted with jewels. Fireplaces larger than her parents' entire cottage burned enormous logs that threw off so much heat the chill of the road was instantly chased away. There was more food and drink than she had ever seen in one place, and there were people everywhere.

Most of the kings and chieftains had arrived that day, so the evening was taken up with feasting and revelry. Maeve would have liked to join in, even if only as a watcher from a corner. But Bradan was too tired for merrymaking and asked that they be shown directly to their chamber. Maeve had to settle for strains of music spiralling up the stone stairwell and glimpses of guests in the courtyard below.

She sighed and picked at the platter of roasted quail and figs on the table. In the chair across from her, Bradan had nodded off, his food untouched. She nudged him gently.

His eyes fluttered open, and he pushed himself upright in his chair.

"Go to bed, Bradan," she said. "You're tired. You need to sleep. Tomorrow is an important day."

"I'm fine," he insisted.

"Go to bed," she said sternly.

The old man patted her hand and dragged himself to his feet. "Yes, yes. You are right. I need to be clear-headed for the council. You should go to bed too," he added as he crawled onto his pallet.

"I will," Maeve replied. "Soon."

And though she did blow out the candle a few minutes later, it was several hours before she was able to sleep.

———

The council chamber was exactly as Bradan had described it in his imaginary dream. High on every wall hung the colourful standards of all the kings and chieftains, and below them was a tangle of angry men yelling at one another. Some shook their fists across a table while others stood toe-to-toe and nose-to-nose, shouting to be heard above the din around them.

From a bench at the back of the room, Maeve observed the proceedings, covering her ears to block out the noise. Bradan had told her to listen to everything, but it was impossible to make sense of this uproar.

She remained watchful, though, and kept her eyes focused on the front of the council chamber. The kings were seated on a low platform above the chieftains, and while they showed more restraint than their lesser counterparts, it was clear they too were quarrelling. No wonder the country was always at war.

King Redmond was the imposing figure in the middle chair. Bradan sat to his left. Maeve was surprised to realize she hardly recognized him. Last evening he'd looked every minute of his age, but now, sitting on the dais and nodding sagely when the king whispered to him, he looked completely at ease and could have been mistaken for royalty. Maeve's gaze moved on. Standing behind King Redmond was a statuesque woman with dark hair and icy grey eyes. Maeve knew it must be Queen Ailsa, though it struck Maeve as odd that she would be attending the war council. None of the other kings had brought their wives.

She watched as the queen made her way to her brother's seat, placed her hand on his shoulder and—when he looked up—discreetly nodded. Then, without a word, she returned to her place behind King Redmond. *And looked straight across the room.* Maeve gasped as the woman's gaze locked on her own. She tried to turn away, but she couldn't. It was as if she were under a spell. It was the queen who finally averted her eyes and released her. Maeve was so relieved she nearly slid off the bench.

King Redmond gestured to the trumpeters, who raised their horns and blew the council chamber into silence.

"Order!" cried the herald. "Let there be order!"

"At this rate we will never form a plan," the king growled. "As your king, I order you to put your personal disagreements aside. We are facing an invasion by bloodthirsty Norsemen who would plunder our castles, murder our children and burn our villages to the ground—all before they've eaten their morning meal. Is that what you want? Because if we don't present a united front to stop them, that is exactly what will happen."

A wave of grumbling rolled through the room. One of the chieftains jumped up. "If I take my men away to fight them Norsemen, Hugh of Ardfert or maybe Laughlan of Cork—or someone else—will swoop in and do exactly what them Norsemen are plannin'. And who'll be there to stop them? Eh?"

Hugh of Ardfert sprang from his chair and snarled in the other man's direction. "Your tiny territory isn't worth the bother, Anlon of Clonard. Besides, it's you what would be tryin' to take advantage of the situation."

Then it was Laughlan of Cork's turn. "I'll thank you not to—"

But that's as far as he got.

"Silence!" bellowed the king.

The assembly immediately quieted, and Maeve watched as the queen leaned forward and whispered in the king's ear. He nodded and then turned to his brother-in-law.

"What say you, Owen?"

The King of Meath got to his feet. He was the male version of his sister, right down to the icy grey eyes. He nodded to King Redmond and smiled. "Sire, is it possible that we are acting in haste?"

The Great King frowned. "What do you mean?"

"Are we absolutely certain there is going to be an attack? How do we know? What is the source of this information? Is it reliable?"

King Redmond's hands tightened on the arms of his chair. "It is," he replied coldly.

"May I ask who the informant is?"

"You may ask, but don't expect an answer. I have no doubt the information is true. As king of this land, there is much I need to know. I have reliable informants everywhere. But I wouldn't if I named them."

King Owen didn't push the matter. "I understand, sire," he said. But Maeve saw a spark of something—irritation, displeasure or frustration perhaps—flash in his eyes. As he sat back down, Maeve noticed Queen Ailsa looking at Bradan

And then the chamber took on a glow. A ray of sunlight burst through a window high above and shone directly down on King Owen. *Was that an omen? What did it mean?* Maeve wondered, for the timing couldn't have been more curious.

"We shall take a few minutes' rest," King Redmond announced. "I am told there is food in the grand hall for those who want it. Give thought to how we should proceed. I wish to have a plan in place by the end of the day. The trumpets will call you back."

CHAPTER 15

The council agreed on a plan of defence before it adjourned, though not without several more heated arguments. The chieftains were to return home, muster their armies and begin the march north, where the Norsemen were expected to land. There they would meet up with their kings and get into position. By sunrise the next day, Castle Carrick—which had bustled with activity the previous day—echoed with emptiness, its guests scattered to the wind like autumn leaves.

It was drizzling when Maeve and Bradan set out to the site of the winter solstice. They took the east road leading to Newgrange in the valley of the Boyne River. Newgrange was a passage tomb built by long-ago farmers. One day each year—on the winter solstice—the rising sun aligned with a small opening in one side, allowing a shaft of light to stream the length of the long passage. The Druids took this as a sign of the coming spring.

Since the winter solstice was only days away, there was no point returning to the Druid camp. It was a longer journey and would be hard on Bradan. Even this short trek was taking its toll.

Maeve frowned as he began coughing—something he'd been doing frequently since they'd left Castle Carrick.

"Rest a while," she said, easing him onto a large rock and handing him the waterskin. She dropped her bundle at his feet and sat down. It was an uncomfortable perch, lumpy and low—her knees were up at her chin—but it was better than sitting on the wet ground.

Bradan was definitely ill. Maeve was worried. She waited for him to stop coughing and said, "You should have accepted King Owen's offer and stayed on at the castle until you were feeling better."

Bradan sighed. "When you become old, there is no *better*. Some days are merely less trying. Stop fussing, child. I will be fine."

Maeve didn't argue. It would only agitate him and drain more of his strength.

"I am looking forward to the winter solstice," she said, "but I can't help feeling guilty about it too. While the Druids are heading to Newgrange for a celebration, everyone else is hurrying north to fight a war."

"Druids are exempt from war," Bradan said. "It goes against our beliefs."

"But you were part of the council of war."

"I am a subject of the king, and he commanded my presence. I could not refuse. Besides, the council wasn't called for the purpose of starting a war, but to protect the land and its people from invasion. There is a difference."

Maeve nodded. "Are you pleased with the outcome?"

"I am satisfied," Bradan replied. "I don't see how it could have gone differently. If the king is to stop the invasion, he must turn the enemy back as soon as its ships touch our shore. Otherwise it will roll over the land like the death machine it is. Then we are all doomed. My biggest worry is that our troops will end up fighting each other instead of the enemy."

Maeve had thought about that too. At the war council, the kings and chieftains hadn't been of one mind regarding how the realm should be defended—or even if it needed to be defended. King Redmond had made the final decision. Everyone pledged their support, but being such a hot-tempered lot, there was no telling what might set them to fighting amongst themselves again.

"Are you one of King Redmond's informants?" Maeve asked.

Bradan raised an eyebrow in surprise. "Why would you ask that?"

"At the council of war, when King Owen was questioning King Redmond about how he knew there was going to be an attack, Queen Ailsa stared straight at you."

"Did she?" Bradan didn't seem overly concerned. "I missed that."

"It was like she wanted everyone to think you were the informant."

Bradan shrugged. "Well, I'm not. I am one of the king's many advisors, but I am not an informant. Perhaps the queen was hoping to discredit me. She is not fond of Druids, and she thinks I have too much influence over the king. So if the Norsemen *don't* invade our land, and people think I said they *would*, King Redmond might stop seeking my counsel."

"I knew I didn't like her," Maeve muttered under her breath. To Bradan she said, "During one of the chieftains' shouting matches, she exchanged a private message with King Owen. She never said a word. She only touched his shoulder and nodded, but I could tell it meant something. Then she whispered in King Redmond's ear, and right after that he called on King Owen to speak."

Bradan nodded. "Yes, I remember her whispering to the king."

"Did you hear what she said?"

"I heard nothing. My ears were still ringing from the rumpus among the chieftains."

Maeve clucked her tongue. "Too bad. I think she's up to something. I don't know what, but I don't trust her."

"Well, she's not someone to be on the wrong side of. That's for certain."

———

Once Bradan was rested and had stopped coughing, they continued on their way. Even though Newgrange wasn't far from Castle Carrick, they went slowly. So they were forced to spend the night on the road—and a cold night it was. Maeve found them shelter within a hollow tree. She softened the ground with pine boughs and built a small fire to ward off the damp and chill. Exhausted from the day's walk, Bradan ate his meal of bread and cheese and fell straight to sleep. Maeve worried that the walking was too much for him, but when he awoke in the morning he seemed better than he had the night before. And so they pushed on. Still, she was glad when they set down their bundles in the valley of the Boyne River.

With help from the Druids who were already assembled, Maeve set up camp and began nursing Bradan back to health. Sleep seemed to be the best medicine, accompanied by hot soup and sweet tea.

"We shall get you feeling like yourself in no time," she said as she snugged a fur rug around him.

Bradan scowled and clucked his tongue. "Don't fuss so. You're like a broody hen."

"Someone has to take care of you. You obviously don't do a good job of it. You push yourself too hard. It's a wonder you've lived this long. You should have a wife to look after you."

He shot her a sideways glance. "Is that a proposal?"

Maeve's mouth dropped open, but she recovered quickly. "Have you ever been married?"

He shook his head.

"Why not? Do you snore? Do you belch and scratch your belly?"

"Do you?" he retorted.

Maeve laughed. "Fair enough." Then she sobered again. "Seriously though, Bradan, why haven't you married? You would've made a fine husband."

He shrugged. "I'm not the marrying sort. Perhaps in my next life."

Maeve drew back in surprise. "Is there another life after this one?"

"Like nature, life is a cycle," Bradan said. "Druids believe that when we leave this life, we are reborn in the otherworld, and when our time is finished there, we are born again into this one. And so it goes."

"It never ends?" When Bradan shook his head, Maeve regarded him curiously. "Why?"

He smiled. "Druids strive to achieve three things in life," he said. "Wisdom, creativity and a love of all things. These are lofty goals and not easily achievable. Being reborn gives us greater opportunity to pursue them."

Maeve sighed and shook her head. "Oh my. I have trouble just understanding myself. I will never master those things no matter how many times I'm reborn."

By the time Declan, Enda and the others arrived, Bradan was almost as hale as he had been before they set out for the war council—except for his cough. That seemed determined to linger.

Maeve stared up at the sky. The night had leaked out of it, but day had not yet arrived to take its place. Still, she could tell it was going to be sunny—cold, but sunny. That was good because it was the winter solstice, and she wanted to see the first rays of sunlight pour into the passage tomb. Standing at its entrance with Enda, Bradan, Finn and Declan, she was in the perfect position.

As the sky became lighter, Newgrange moved out of the shadows so that Maeve could finally see it properly. It was a massive mound of earth, extending beyond her vision and standing ten men high. Huge stones bearing intricately carved symbols were lined up around it. The tomb passage ran beneath, through the centre, from front to back. The passage was dark now, but soon the sun would stream through the tiny window at the rear. Maeve could hardly contain her excitement.

She turned her gaze to the horizon. This was her first winter solstice with the Druids, and she didn't want to miss the precise moment of its arrival. Barely remembering to breathe, she watched unblinking as the sun's first rays spilled across the rolling meadow like molten gold. Now that it had broken through, the sun climbed faster, impatient to be fully born.

And then it happened. The passageway, which seconds before had been dark, was blazing with sunlight. Maeve could see the giant stones lining the tunnel's sides, as well as the chamber partway along that contained the bones and ashes of the dead.

A unified gasp of awe went up from the assembled Druids, and Maeve hugged Bradan's arm. She felt strangely exhilarated. Though her feet were on the ground, she felt like she was floating. It was as if a part of her she hadn't known existed had been awakened, and light was streaming through her just as it streamed through the tunnel.

"Well?" Bradan said as they made their way back to the encampment.

"It was wonderful," Maeve sighed dreamily. "I can't believe it happens but one day a year."

"That is the wonder of it," he replied. "But the best is yet to come."

And so it was.

Later that day, all the Druids met in a nearby grove. They wore wreaths of ivy in their hair and berry garlands round their necks. In their hands they carried holly and baskets of pine cones, acorns, chestnuts and oak leaves. One of the elders gave thanks to the gods for a fruitful cycle of seasons. As he spoke, Maeve watched two white bulls, which were secured to stakes just beyond the circle of Druids. Never before had she seen anything like them.

It wasn't long before her gaze wandered from the bulls to the sky. After ushering in the solstice, the sun had withdrawn behind a steadily growing bank of clouds, which was now an iron-grey blanket pushing down on the treetops.

As Maeve marvelled at nature's glory, thinking the day couldn't get any better, it began to snow. At first a few fine flakes fell softly on her cheeks and forehead like gentle prickles of cold, melting almost the instant they touched her skin. But then they came faster and heavier until a fine dusting covered the ground.

Maeve pulled herself from her thoughts and focused once more on the Druid elder. He was standing beneath a tall oak tree. Even robbed of its leaves, the tree was majestic, but it was the fat, green mistletoe hanging heavily from a low branch that held her attention.

As she watched, the elder raised a golden sickle. With one sweep of his arm he severed the plant from the tree. Another Druid caught it in a white cloth and everyone cheered. Then, before Maeve could comprehend what was happening, the two white bulls were given to the gods with thanks, and Master Finn recited a special poem he'd composed for the occasion.

When night fell, there was one final tribute to the day. A mighty yule log was set ablaze to chase away the bleakness of winter and encourage the speedy arrival of spring.

"This celebration happens every year?" Maeve said to Enda as they made their way back to the encampment in the moonlight.

Enda nodded. "It's magical, isn't it?" she sighed. And then, "Oh, I just remembered. Your sister—"

Maeve turned quickly to her friend, the solstice forgotten. "What about her?"

"She came by the camp before we left. She was asking after you."

"Was she all right?"

Enda shrugged. "She seemed fine. A bit jumpy perhaps. Anyway, I told her you were with Bradan, but that I would be seeing you soon. She said I was to tell you that you have been much in her thoughts, and she was wondering if you would come to be with her in the spring when her baby arrives."

Maeve was stunned. She hadn't realized how much she had missed Deirdre, and how she had pushed thoughts of her away to avoid the hurt. But now Deirdre was reaching out. Maeve didn't know why now when she hadn't before, but it didn't matter. Her heart was full. "Thank you," she said and squeezed Enda's hand.

When Maeve and Enda arrived at the encampment, the others were already there. And they weren't alone. Two strangers in royal livery were talking with Bradan. The local king's men, Maeve thought. She was curious to know what business had brought them.

At the sound of the young women's approach, one of them turned, and Maeve froze. The front of his tunic was emblazoned with King Redmond's crest. That could mean only one thing.

Chapter 16

As Maeve suspected, Bradan was once again being summoned. King Redmond had had a troubling dream, which he was anxious for Bradan to explain.

"But it's at least three days' travel to his castle," Maeve protested, "and you are not yet well."

Bradan began to cough.

"You see!" she cried. "It's cold—and getting colder. And it's snowing, Bradan! You can't travel in these conditions. You'll get sicker than you already are."

"I have no choice," he said. "The king has summoned me."

"But he doesn't know you're ill. We could send him a message and—"

"Stop," he said wearily. "I am going. Are you coming with me or not?"

Maeve wished she could find the words to change the old Druid's mind, but she knew the fight was already lost. "Of course I'm coming. You can't go alone," she muttered crossly.

"Good. We leave at daybreak."

"I think Enda should come too," Maeve blurted. Before Bradan could object, she hurried on. "She is a wonder with herbs. If anyone can tend to your cough, it's Enda. And she can make wholesome soups to warm you. With both of us working together, the journey will be more comfortable."

"Maeve is right," Enda jumped in. "Let me come along, Bradan."

"Me as well," Declan said, catching Maeve by surprise. "I am young and strong. You can lean on me when the going becomes difficult. If needs be, I can plough a path through the snow, snare a rabbit for our supper and find us shelter. With three of us to help you, we can ensure you get to the king quickly and in good health."

Bradan looked at the eager faces of the young people. Maeve couldn't tell what he was thinking, nor what his answer would be. It was some time before he spoke, but finally he sighed. "Very well."

———

Maeve had mixed feelings about Declan joining them on the journey. He would be a great help, but she was uneasy about being so much in his company.

They left as soon as it was light enough, and to Maeve's immense relief, Bradan wasn't forced to walk. Declan had spoken to Finn, who had spoken to a local farmer, who had given them the loan of a donkey. So Bradan could ride. That would speed up their trek and also be less taxing on the old seer.

The journey started off well enough. Though there was a nip to the air, the snow had stopped falling and the sun was shining, so the going was relatively easy. Along the way they met up with a chieftain and his clansmen also making their way north, though no one seemed to know precisely where they were going. But their spirits were high as they waved clubs and cudgels, spears, and swords—those who had them—and boasted of the drubbing they would give the Norsemen.

At a crossroad, the sometime soldiers veered northwest to join up with another troop, while Bradan and company continued up the north-eastern road that led to King Redmond's castle.

Shortly after they parted ways with the soldiers, a bitterly cold wind blew up from the north, bring-ing snow. It whipped at their cloaks and hurled ice pellets into their faces. Even pulling their mantles close and huddling into their hoods, they were soon chilled to the bone. At one point they sought shelter behind an embankment, but not even that could save them from the wind and cold. By the time they stopped for the night, Maeve had lost all feeling in her hands and feet. Her fingers wouldn't even move to untie the knot of her bundle.

How Declan managed to start a fire was beyond her, but as soon as it was lit, they set a log in front of it and helped Bradan to sit. Enda got straight to work melting snow for tea and soup, while Declan set off to gather firewood.

Maeve laid a fur over Bradan's knees and another around his shoulders. Then she took one of his hands between her own and began rubbing it briskly to bring the feeling back.

"Are you getting any warmer?" she asked. Her own hands had started to burn as the heat from the fire thawed them. She took up Bradan's other hand and gave it a good rub too.

"Thank you, child. The fire will warm me. Don't fret so."

Enda arrived with wooden bowls of hot tea. Maeve blew on hers and drank greedily. The soothing liquid slid down her throat, warming her steadily from the inside out.

"Drink, Bradan," she urged him. "It's warm and good."

The old man took a sip but then lowered the bowl again and stared blankly into the fire.

It was as Maeve had feared. This journey was proving too much for him.

The next day was no better. The wind blew as hard as ever, whirling the snow into deep drifts that blocked their way. Declan and Maeve were constantly having to carve pathways through them.

Though Bradan didn't complain, it seemed to Maeve that he was shrinking before her eyes, nearly doubled over on the donkey and looking as if he were going to slide off at any moment.

She tugged on Declan's arm. "We have to stop," she said. "Right now. I don't care that it's only mid-afternoon. Bradan can't go on. This journey is killing him."

Declan looked at the old man. When his gaze shifted back to Maeve, his forehead was buckled with concern and his mouth stretched into a tight line. He nodded. Then he squinted into the snow blowing round them and pointed to a small woodland off their path. A huge drift had formed on the north side of it, but under the trees themselves there was hardly any snow. The ground was even bare in spots.

"We'll be sheltered from the wind there," he said. "It isn't ideal, but it will be better than being completely in the open."

———

Bradan was barely conscious when they wrapped him in furs and laid him on a bed of pine boughs by the fire. Enda immediately began spooning a brew of something pungent and very green into his mouth, ignoring the old man's feeble attempts to push it away.

"Don't fight me, Bradan," she said sternly. "This will help you, and whether you like it or not, I'm going to see that you get better."

Maeve smiled grimly. She was counting on her friend to do exactly that. No one knew herbs and their powers better than Enda. If Bradan's health could be restored, she was the one to do it. But he was so sick. Maeve despaired to see him shudder with cold, his eyes dark and sunken in his pale face. Perhaps he was too weak already—even for Enda's skills.

Declan cut into her thoughts. "I'm going to build a shelter here under the trees. It's stopped snowing, but we still need to protect Bradan from the wind."

"I'll help you," Maeve said, trying to shake off the depression she was sinking into. It was better to do something useful than to worry.

"Why don't you gather wood?" Declan replied. "We're going to need a lot of it if we're to keep the fire burning through the night."

Maeve nodded and got to work.

At first she foraged the immediate area, returning every few minutes with arms full of kindling, small branches and even a few decent-sized logs. The pile was growing, but they were going to need much, much more.

As she expanded her search, she changed her tactic. Instead of returning to the camp with each load, she began dropping the wood in a central location to be relayed to the camp later. This let her conserve her energy instead of exhausting herself carrying heavy loads long distances.

But it was a small woodland, and as she ventured farther, the trees began to thin out, replaced by outcroppings of rock dotted with bushes and only the occasional evergreen. Maeve wanted to collect as much firewood as she could, so she began scrambling over and around the rocks and boulders to get to the isolated trees. She was surprised to find several large pieces of dead wood lying in the snow. Picking up one after the other without paying heed to where she was going, she soon found herself standing at the entrance to a cave. It took her a moment to realize that's what it was because the opening was partly hidden by a craggy mass of boulders.

Maeve couldn't believe her luck. A cave was the perfect place to make camp for the night. There would be no snow, no wind, and the heat of a fire built in the entrance would be contained by the cave walls instead of being sucked into the open air.

As she started to hurry back and tell the others, a chunk of wood slid from her arms. She bent to pick it up and then changed her mind. There was no point taking this firewood with her. She'd only have to carry it back again. She decided to leave it at the entrance to the cave.

As she was dropping the logs, something red in the snow, just inside the cave mouth, caught her eye. She hunkered down for a closer look.

It was blood.

CHAPTER 17

Maeve's heart began to race. There was someone—or something—inside the cave. And whoever or whatever it was was injured or had drawn blood.

She jumped up and looked around her. The snow outside the cave entrance was pristine white. No blood there. But it was also deeper than the snow in the mouth of the cave, which meant it was fresher. Maeve swept away the newer snow with her boot.

And there it was.

She moved away from the cave and dug into another patch of snow. More blood.

She didn't know what to do. If the blood belonged to an animal, she needed to get as far away as possible. There was nothing more dangerous than a wounded badger or fox. But if it was an injured person inside the cave, she should try to help.

Cautiously, Maeve made her way back to the entrance and—tensing to run if necessary—peeked into the darkness. "Hello?" She cocked her head and listened. Hearing nothing, she took another step into the cave and called again. "Is someone in here?"

"*Stop!*" a voice inside her head boomed.

Maeve froze.

"*Don't come any farther.*"

"*Riasc Tiarna?*" Maeve thought back to the voice.

"*It is I.*"

Relief washed over her, and then she remembered the blood in the snow. "*You're hurt,*" she said, starting into the cave once more.

"*I told you to stop! Do you not know the meaning of the word?*"

Maeve growled under her breath. Druids and dragons could be so difficult. "*Of course I do,*" she thought back crossly. "*But I want to help. You're bleeding.*"

"*I was bleeding. I'm not anymore. It was merely a scratch.*"

Maeve didn't believe him. "*What happened to you?*"

"*I paid a visit to my old friend, the black dragon, on the other side of the northern sea. He wasn't very hospitable.*"

Maeve knew Riasc Tiarna was being sarcastic—the black dragon was not his friend. Why would he go there? And then it dawned on her.

"*You went to see if the Norsemen were preparing to attack,*" she thought to him.

She waited for his answer, but her head remained quiet.

"*You are the king's informant, aren't you?*" she pushed. And when he still didn't respond, she taunted him. "*I know you are. There's no point denying it. There is no other reason for you to cross the sea, and no one else who could discover the Norsemen are manning their ships—and still return in time to warn the king.*"

To Maeve's surprise, chuckling filled her head.

"*You are getting too clever,*" Riasc Tiarna told her. "*The old Druid has taught you well. That is good. You are going to need every skill you possess.*"

"*What do you mean?*" Maeve asked, suddenly wary.

"*The time has almost arrived for you to make the decision I told you of—the decision that will affect the lives of many. I trust you are ready. Know that the responsibility rests on your shoulders, but you won't have to act alone. You will have help—if you choose to use it.*"

"*It sounds like you already know I shall accept the challenge.*"

"*As I said before—only you can choose your path.*"

Maeve allowed herself a harsh laugh. "*Why do I have the feeling my choice won't really be a choice at all?*"

"*I would not lie to you.*"

"*But you would toy with me. You and Bradan are playing a game. You both know more than I do, but you are particular about what you share. It's as if you are steering me along a path, though you try to make me believe I am choosing my own way.*"

"*Because you are. You are a child of the forest. You know what hides among the trees. You need only look within and trust what you see.*"

Maeve sighed. "*Another riddle.*"

"*You have been long away from your friends. You should get back,*" Riasc Tiarna replied.

Maeve still had many questions, but a wall had gone up inside her head. She knew Riasc Tiarna was on the other side of it. She also knew that he had raised the wall, and she wouldn't be able to break through it no matter how hard she tried. So she picked up the scattered pieces of firewood and headed back to her friends. She had to tell Bradan what she'd discovered.

The old man was sleeping when she reached the camp. It wasn't a restful slumber though. His limbs flailed, his brow was furrowed and he was muttering. Where his skin had been deathly pale before, it was now feverishly red. Enda was at his side, dabbing his face and neck with a wet rag.

"How is he?" Maeve asked.

Enda shook her head. "Very sick."

"But he's going to get better, isn't he?"

"I shall do my best to see to it."

Maeve wrinkled her nose. "What's that smell?"

Enda smiled. "Onion. I made a poultice for his chest. It will help loosen the congestion. Of course, that means no onion in the soup, but—" She shrugged.

Since Maeve couldn't speak with Bradan, she went back to work fetching the wood she'd left deeper in the trees. It took several trips, and it was dark by the time she set down the last load.

Bradan awoke with a fit of coughing.

"Maeve," he called when it had subsided. His voice was a raspy croak.

She hurried to where he lay. Declan left off his work on the shelter and joined them.

"I am not going to be able to reach the king," Bradan said.

"Don't talk like that," Maeve admonished him. "Of course—"

"Don't interrupt, child," he wheezed. "For once, just listen."

Maeve bit her lip and took the old man's hand in her own. She silently scolded herself for her thoughtlessness. Because he was so weak, it was difficult for Bradan to speak, and she was only adding to the strain. "I'm sorry," she apologized.

"You must go in my place."

Maeve stared at him in disbelief. He couldn't be serious. The king wanted a dream explained. She didn't have the skills for that. Perhaps someday she would, but not now—not yet. Bradan must realize that, and it wouldn't take the king long to figure it out either. He would see through the charade in an instant. Then he'd lock her away in his castle and let her rot. That's if she could even find her way to his castle.

No, this was not going to work. Maeve opened her mouth to tell Bradan so and then shut it again. He was once more struggling to speak.

"I know you don't think you can do it, but you can. I have faith in you. Have I been wrong yet?" He allowed himself a small chuckle, which immediately turned into another bout of coughing.

When it had passed, he took a few moments to allow his wheezing to ease. Then he raised a shaky hand to his neck. "The chain, Enda—help me get it off."

Enda lifted it over his head and let it curl into his open hand.

Bradan held it out to Maeve. "Take it. It was a gift from the king many years ago. Show it to him and say the words—*and so we are linked*. He will remember and know you come at my bidding."

"But—" Maeve began.

Bradan lifted a finger to his lips to quiet her. "I sense the king's dream will affect the outcome of the Norsemen's attack. That is why you must go. You must discover its meaning. I know you are afraid. That is to be expected. But you can do this. Remember what I've taught you. Listen to your heart and your head. And believe in yourself." He smiled and patted her hand.

How could she say no? This was what she'd been training for. But she wasn't ready!

Maeve felt her backbone stiffen. She *would* do this. She didn't know how, but she would. She had to. If Bradan had faith in her, she wouldn't let him down. She slipped the chain round her neck.

Bradan's gaze shifted to Declan. "You will go with Maeve. She may have need of you. Also, this is a momentous time, and the story of it will need telling. It is your responsibility as a bard to pass on the tale."

Declan nodded. "As you wish, Bradan. But what of you and Enda? How will you manage?"

It was Enda who answered. "I can do more than brew tea, young Declan. I'll take care of us, don't you fret."

Maeve hadn't told Bradan about crossing paths with Riasc Tiarna while she'd been gathering firewood, but there was no point in bringing it up now. The old man already suspected matters were coming to a head. Having confirmation would only worry him, and he already had enough troubles.

CHAPTER 18

Before Declan bedded down that night, he set a snare, and when he checked it the next morning he discovered a large rabbit. Maeve was thankful and relieved. It meant that Bradan wouldn't starve while they were away, and that gave her one less thing to worry about.

Bradan was still asleep as the two young people prepared to leave, so they said their good-byes to Enda and set out on the last leg of the journey to King Redmond's castle. Declan took the lead while Maeve followed behind. The crust on the snow's surface crunched beneath their boots, and they moved in synchronized rhythm, both lost in their thoughts.

When the sun finally broke on the horizon, its rays splintered the snow like shards of ice, and despite her preoccupation with the king's dream, Maeve gasped at the wonder of it. It was the sort of natural splendour she relished, and for a few moments it took her mind off the impossible task that lay ahead.

Declan stopped and waited for her to catch up, squinting against the brilliance of the sun on the snow.

"Isn't it glorious?" Maeve sighed when she reached him.

"If blinding is glorious. I can barely keep my eyes open."

"My eyes are watering too," Maeve admitted, "but I don't mind. It's beautiful." She gazed skyward. Everywhere she looked it was blue. "It's going to be a fine day," she said. "Thank goodness. I don't think I could bear more awful weather."

Declan closed his eyes and turned his face to the sun. "I can already feel the warmth. This will melt the snow. If we keep up a good pace, we'll reach the castle before nightfall."

Maeve had mixed feelings about that. It could mean she would get to sleep in a comfortable bed. Or it could mean the king would discover she was an imposter and clap her in irons.

"Maeve?" Declan's voice penetrated her thoughts, and she realized her mind had been wandering.

She shook her head to clear it. "Sorry. What did you say?"

"It's not important. You were worrying about Bradan, weren't you?"

A wave of guilt washed over her. She *was* concerned about Bradan, though it was her own problems she was thinking about at the moment. "Yes, but—"

Before she could finish, Declan pulled her into a hug. It happened so quickly, and Maeve was so surprised, she didn't resist. Then, without realizing it, she wrapped her arms around his waist.

"You are amazing," Declan mumbled into her hair. "You're living among strangers who demand impossible things, and still your greatest concern is the welfare of others. Bradan is very ill. I know that worries you, but he's stronger than he seems, and Enda is a powerful healer. There's nothing you can do for him right now, so you must have faith and try not to think about it."

Maeve's guilty feelings came pouring back. She pulled away and looked up at Declan, trying to decide whether or not to dispel his flattering—but flawed—assessment of her. "I am not amazing," she said at last. "But I am lucky. The Druids took me in when I had nowhere else to go. Yes, you were strangers, once. But that seems like a lifetime ago. Now you are my friends—no, my family. Bradan is like a father to me. Of course I care what happens to him." She took a breath, and though she was embarrassed to admit it, she said, "But just now I was worrying about myself."

"Why? What's wrong?"

Maeve turned away and gazed into the distance. "In a few hours our Great King is going to ask me to explain his dream—a dream that could determine the outcome of the invasion. I've never interpreted a dream before." She spun back toward Declan. "What if I get it wrong? Thousands of people could be slaughtered, and I'll be to blame. It'll be my fault! I couldn't live with that."

The memory of Riasc Tiarna's words echoed in her head. *"Know that someone—indeed a great many people—are going to need your help. The task will seem impossible.*" This was what he'd been speaking of. He may have warned her, but she certainly wasn't prepared.

For a few seconds, Declan said nothing. He stared at Maeve, though she could tell he wasn't seeing her. He was looking past her at the enormity of what she'd said.

Finally his eyes refocused. "You may never have interpreted a dream before, but that doesn't mean you can't do it. Bradan has faith in you. I do too. When the time comes, you will do what needs doing—that's who you are."

Maeve thought her heart was going to jump out of her chest. She hugged Declan again. "Thank you." She wasn't convinced what he'd said was true, but it was reassuring to hear.

As they started walking again, Maeve felt lighter—happier. She was still anxious about what lay ahead, but things between Declan and her had been repaired. She hadn't realized how much their falling out had weighed on her until they resolved it. And because Declan had made the first move to fix things, she wanted him to know how she felt.

"Last autumn when I learned why you'd been taking me to the Druid camp, I was angry," she said. "I thought you'd been dishonest with me. Bradan said you were only doing what he'd asked, and I shouldn't blame you. But I felt I couldn't trust you anymore. So I've been avoiding you."

"I could tell," Declan said quietly. "I'm sure everyone else could too."

Maeve lowered her eyes. "I'm sorry. I should have talked to you, but I was embarrassed. If I hadn't been so stubborn, we could have worked things out a lot sooner." She swept her arm through the air in a gesture of dismissal. "But never mind. That's all behind us now. The important thing is we're still friends."

———

They arrived at King Redmond's castle as the sun was sliding behind the hills. As they stood at the outer wall, banging the knocker on the massive oak door, a sentry in the gatehouse above stuck out his head and barked, "Who goes there? What is your business?"

"We are Druids—a seer and her escort, here at the bidding of the king," Declan replied.

Maeve sent him a sideways glance. Why had he said that? He was a Druid, but she wasn't. She supposed it was probably easier to say that than explain how a commoner might be a seer.

The sentry grumbled something and disappeared inside the gatehouse. Several minutes later he reappeared. "Away with you, or be thrown into irons."

"We have business with the king," Declan protested.

"Not according to the queen," the sentry shouted back.

"Let us in and I shall prove we speak the truth," Maeve called to him.

The sentry hooted disparagingly. "I don't take orders from children." Then he sobered again and snarled, "You heard me. Be gone!"

"You are either a very brave man or a very foolish one," Maeve blustered, not caring what consequences her bold words might have. She had an important job to do, and she was not about to let anyone stop her from doing it. "When the king discovers we were here and you turned us away, your neck and shoulders will most certainly part company."

"Are you trying to get us killed?" Declan whispered before addressing the gatekeeper. "We have no reason to lie about our intentions, sir. Perhaps the queen is unaware the king sent for a seer. Tell him we have a message from Bradan the Druid. I guarantee he will see us." When the man didn't reply, he added, "The king will be grateful for your loyal service."

Once again the sentry disappeared. After a time a voice on the other side of the door barked an order. Then there was much clanging and banging as the bolts were thrown back, the iron bar was pulled aside and the enormous door was dragged open, groaning mightily on its hinges. There would be no sneaking into this castle, Maeve decided.

"You catch more flies with honey than vinegar," Declan told her under his breath as they were ushered inside by several of the king's men.

"You think it was *you* who convinced him to let us in?" Maeve hissed back.

Declan shrugged.

"It doesn't matter which of us changed his mind," she conceded. "The important thing is we are going to see the king."

"Or perhaps we're on our way to the gallows," Declan countered with a straight face. "In which case, this was all your doing."

Maeve was glad he had his hand beneath her arm, because her legs chose that precise moment to cease holding her up.

CHAPTER 19

At first Maeve tried to memorize the route the king's men were taking, but they turned so many corners, walked so many halls and climbed so many stairs she soon gave up. If she had to run for her life, she would be lost in the castle forever. But she wasn't alone, she reminded herself. Declan was with her, and he was resourceful. He would have plotted their escape while they were still outside the castle walls.

Finally they came to a halt in front of a pair of heavy doors in a dark hallway somewhere deep in the castle. Sentries were positioned on each side of the entrance. At the group's approach they blocked the doors with their spears.

"Druids to see the king. They are expected," said the lead guard escorting Maeve and Declan.

The sentries nodded and one of them banged his spear on the door.

It immediately opened and another sentry appeared. The message was once more relayed, the sentry within the chamber nodded and the door closed.

Maeve and Declan exchanged glances. It was no small feat gaining an audience with the king.

While they waited, the silence was so oppressive Maeve felt the stone walls closing in on her. In a matter of minutes she would be asked to explain the king's dream—a dream that, if interpreted correctly, could save the land from unimaginable bloodshed. But if misinterpreted... Maeve shuddered. She couldn't think of that. Bradan and Riasc Tiarna had told her to believe in herself. Despite their faith in her, Maeve was terrified she would fail.

She tried distracting herself with the dancing light of the torches, but it cast such eerie shadows, her imagination began to run amok. As if sensing her rising panic, Declan squeezed her hand, and she willed herself back to calm.

At last the door opened slightly, and to Maeve's surprise the queen moved into the opening. She glared at the guards. "Does no one obey orders? I thought I'd made myself clear. The king is not to be disturbed. Take these two away."

Maeve would have protested—regardless of Declan's warning tug on her hand—but before she had the chance, the door opened fully, revealing the king. The startled expression on his face indicated that Maeve and Declan were not who he was expecting to see.

"You needn't concern yourself, sire." The queen tried to hurry him back into the chamber. "I can deal with this."

It was as if the king hadn't heard. He pushed past her into the hall. "Where is the seer? The Druid?" he said, confusion furrowing his brow. "Where is Bradan?"

Seeing her chance, Maeve spoke quickly. "He is ill, sire. I am his apprentice. He sent me to explain your dream in his stead." She slipped the chain from around her neck and held it out. "He said you would remember this gift and know I come in good faith. *And so we are linked.*"

For a very long moment King Redmond's gaze travelled back and forth between Maeve and the chain, assessing the truth of things. Finally he nodded. "Yes. I remember you were with Bradan at the council of war. He is one of my most loyal subjects. If he hasn't come as I asked, he must be ill indeed. This is unwelcome news." He frowned and beckoned them into the chamber.

Maeve had assumed the room would be large — everything else in the castle was. But it was a small space, containing only a few chairs and a table covered with parchments. Bent over them was King Owen. As they entered, he looked up.

The king gestured toward his brother-in-law. "We have been working on our defence. My informant tells me the Norsemen are on their way."

Riasc Tiarna, Maeve thought, though she said nothing.

"We must get our armies into position and be quick about it," the king continued. "Unfortunately, they have not yet all arrived. We have my men, of course, as well as King Owen's clansmen from the Midlands, but we are still waiting on the troops from the most eastern and western regions as well as all of the south. I was counting on Bradan to explain my dream so we can position ourselves to best advantage until reinforcements arrive." He paused, and as his gaze turned to Maeve, she could see his confidence waver. "You are but a child. How can you have the skills to parse the meaning of my dream?"

It was clear he wanted to believe, but he was doubtful. Maeve swallowed hard. She knew exactly how he felt.

"Bradan wouldn't have sent me if I couldn't interpret your dream, sire." It was a bold state-ment—bolder than she felt. But she knew it was true. Bradan *wouldn't* have sent her in his place if he was unsure. She tried to muster conviction from that. She thought of her last meeting with Riasc Tiarna. He had told her to be brave. She pulled back her shoulders and stood tall. It didn't chase away her doubts, but it helped put her in a frame of mind to try.

The queen clucked her tongue. "As you have pointed out, sire, the girl is but a child." She looked Maeve up and down. "Thirteen years, I would say." When Maeve confirmed her assess-ment with a bob of her head, the queen smiled, but it was an icy gesture. "I thought so," she said. Then she turned back to the king. "Sire, are you willing to risk the fate of your kingdom on the word of one so young? Perhaps it is best to follow King Owen's plan. He has presented a sound strategy."

"Yes, yes, of course," King Redmond replied impatiently, "but first I would like to have my dream explained. It may show us something we haven't thought of. The dream is important. I feel it in my bones."

Maeve could see Queen Ailsa disagreed, but it was also clear King Redmond was not going to be dissuaded. The queen had no choice but to give way. Though Maeve had no liking for the woman, she was impressed by how graciously Queen Ailsa backed down. "Of course, sire. As you wish. My concern is time. We have so little, we can't afford to squander it."

The king smiled and patted her hand. "Let us begin then," he said.

Chairs were brought forward for Maeve and the king. Declan gave Maeve's shoulder a squeeze before stepping back into the shadows.

Sitting directly across from the king, Maeve tried to get comfortable—an impossible task considering where she was, who she was with and what she had to do. The moment of truth had arrived. *Stay calm,* she told herself.

But as her mind formed the thought, her body tensed and panic took root in her stomach. She stopped breathing, her ears began to ring and her head and stomach started to whirl. Was she going to be sick? A shudder shook her body. She looked at the king. His lips were moving, but there was no sound. *How could she interpret his dream when she couldn't hear him!*

She slumped into the chair and closed her eyes. Declan was immediately at her side, his hand on her arm, his voice steady and reassuring in her ear. The ringing subsided.

"Breathe," Declan was saying. "Take deep breaths. And relax. You're all right. You can do this, Maeve."

And suddenly it wasn't Declan speaking to her. It was Bradan. He was telling her to breathe deeply and let herself go, to relax and open her senses, to free her mind and heart and to believe in herself.

Maeve opened her eyes and offered Declan a shaky smile. "Thank you," she said. "I'm fine now." She took another deep breath and let it out slowly.

"Are you sure?"

She nodded. "Yes." Then she turned to King Redmond. "I'm sorry, sire. I'm a simple country girl, and this is a bit overwhelming—the castle, your presence—" She spread her arms to take everything in. "I'm afraid my nerves got the better of me. But I'm fine now."

King Redmond looked concerned. "You're certain? Perhaps the queen is right. Perhaps this is too much for you."

It is! Maeve wanted to cry. She was trying to put on a brave front, but she was overwhelmed with fear and doubt. There was so much at stake. So many people's lives hung in the balance. It was too much pressure. She couldn't do this.

From the corner of her eye, Maeve could see the queen preparing to swoop in and take control.

Despite her fear, Maeve couldn't let that happen. "No, no," she said quickly. "It was only a touch of nerves, and I assure you it has passed. We mustn't lose any more time. Tell me your dream, sire."

The king looked unsure but sat back in his chair, shut his eyes and began again. "The place in my dream is the valley north of this castle, though in my dream it looked different. It was as lush and green as ever it has been, but there was an apple orchard. It was a small grove—only eight trees, but they were fine, majestic trees, strong and broad, and heavy with fruit. Flitting among them was a butterfly. It was an idyllic place, and it warmed me and filled my heart with joy."

As King Redmond spoke, Maeve took deep breaths to keep her panic at bay while she tried to concentrate on the scene growing in her mind.

"But then a debilitating cold seeped through," the king continued, "and a great, green snake slithered into the orchard. I almost didn't see it, for it blended with the grass. The butterfly alerted me to its presence. It hovered over the snake, following as it wound itself around each tree. And when the serpent finally left by the same route it had come, the butterfly went with it. After it was gone, only seven trees remained in the orchard.

"I was saddened—not because the snake had left, but because the butterfly had left with it and the orchard was diminished. As I watched them go, I could see in the distance a black cloud of crows moving steadily toward the orchard."

The king opened his eyes. "That is my dream. I know not what it means, but the sense of loss it stirs in me runs deep. I am certain it is an omen of something terrible to come." He paused and regarded Maeve hopefully. "Can you explain it, seer?"

Maeve barely noticed that the king had called her *seer*. She was too caught up in his dream. When he'd begun, she had chanted over and over in her head the things Bradan had told her to do — relax, listen, use your senses, think, weigh all the parts, trust your intuition and the truth will show itself. Merely attempting to remember so many things was overwhelming, and Maeve felt her mind and body becoming tense again. She knew that tension would block the sense of the dream from reaching her, so she cleared her head, like a broom sweeping everything away, and let the king's words fall on the bare floor of her mind.

But it did no good. Try as she might, she could not make sense of the dream. She saw the orchard, its trees heavy with fruit; saw too the blue of the sky and felt the warmth of the sun. She watched the butterfly float on the breeze. And as the snake slithered into the orchard, she shuddered with dread. She felt its evil, but she didn't know what it meant. Her mind was empty. The one time she needed it to see things others could not, her head had forsaken her.

Bradan had been wrong. She couldn't do this! Panic threatened to take her down.

"Seer?" the king urged when several minutes passed without her uttering a word.

Maeve closed her eyes and slowly lifted a finger in a plea for more time. She hoped she looked calm, though her thoughts were racing. Bradan's teachings were a jumble in her mind. The dragon's words from their first meeting came to her. "*When the time arrives, you will be prepared. Have faith. And be brave.*"

The Druid and the dragon had told her to believe in herself. In desperation she peered deep within, searching for something—anything—that might help her understand the king's dream. Riasc Tiarna had said she was a child of the forest, as if that would help her solve the dream. "*You know what hides among the trees. You need only look within and trust what you see.*"

Was the forest the key? When Bradan had told her to walk through the forest in her mind, she had become one with it. Since she could think of no other solution, she went there once more. Almost instantly her mind returned to the peaceful state she had experienced that day.

She replayed the king's dream in her head again. This time, with each word of its telling, it became not only the king's dream, but hers as well. She knew at once what it meant. *You know what hides among the trees.*

Yes, she did. A wave of relief washed over her.

"Sire," she said as she opened her eyes, "what lies to the north of this valley in your dream?"

"Hills—and beyond them the northern sea. But there is a gap in the hills, and it is through this opening the Norsemen will come. This is where we will make our stand. If we can keep the enemy from getting past the hills, our land will be safe."

"Is there another way to get past the hills?" Maeve asked.

"Sire!" There was a sharp urgency to King Owen's voice. "Surely it is unwise to share your battle strategies with this girl. How do you know she isn't a spy, fishing for information?"

The king turned to his brother-in-law. "I appreciate your concern, Owen, but you needn't worry on that account. The girl has been sent by the Druid. If she has his trust, she has mine."

"Sire, you have a good heart, but perhaps you are too tru—" began the queen, but King Redmond cut her off.

"I will hear the girl," he said, the iron in his voice unmistakable. He turned his attention back to Maeve. "Ask your question again, child."

"Is there another way through the hills?"

The king's brow furrowed in thought. "Yes," he said, though he seemed unsure. "The hills stretch far to the west, where they career together in sharp, treacherous mountains of rock. A path winds through their steep walls. But it is wide enough to accommodate only three—perhaps four—men walking abreast. It would take some time for an army to pass through, and the cliffs above the passage provide the perfect stand for an ambush." He shook his head. "The Norsemen aren't fools. They wouldn't come that way."

"Even if they knew it would be undefended?" Maeve asked.

The king was clearly caught off guard. "How could they know that?"

Maeve sighed. "Your dream is a warning of treachery."

"The snake?" the king said.

Maeve nodded. "Someone in your ranks has turned against you. One of the kings, I think. Your orchard had eight trees—the number of kings in this land, excluding yourself. But after the snake visits, only seven remain. In your dream, from what direction do the crows come?"

"The west."

"If I recall correctly, this is where the narrow opening in the hills can be found. The crows represent the Norsemen, and they are going to invade your land through that gateway. One of your kings has told them it will be unguarded."

Before the king could react, there was a loud pounding on the chamber doors. As everyone turned toward the sound, the doors flew open and a messenger burst in, gasping for air.

"Sire," he panted, "I have ridden hard the whole way back from the northern sea. I have news! The Norsemen have landed and begun their march south. They will reach the pass in the hills by morning."

CHAPTER 20

"There is no time to lose," King Owen cried, rushing to the table and snatching up the parchments. "We must get our troops into position. With your permission, sire, I shall rally our armies and dispatch them to the eastern portal of the valley with all speed."

King Redmond put up a hand to stay him. "Not yet. My dream indicates a change of plan is called for. We need to think on this."

"If we don't act now, the enemy will breach the gap and all will be lost!" King Owen argued.

"If that indeed is where the Norsemen intend to attack."

"Surely you don't believe the girl's story," the queen scoffed. "It is a child's flight of fancy. It makes no sense. Please, sire. I beseech you. Don't be fooled by her act. I have a bad feeling about her."

I don't wonder, Maeve thought. She had told King Redmond there was a traitor in the ranks, though she hadn't said who. She also hadn't told him that the traitor had an accomplice. She sensed he wouldn't believe that his queen and her brother were plotting against him, and she feared that if she told him, he might reject her explanation of his dream. Since the important thing was to change the battle plan, Maeve thought it best to keep the identity of the traitors to herself—for now.

The king frowned at Queen Ailsa. "Why do you mistrust her, my dear? Bradan sent her. Is that not proof of her loyalty? What would she gain by lying?"

Though the queen continued to bluster and protest, she could put forward no sound argument to change his mind.

"I'm not suggesting we divert all our troops to the western hills," the king said, "but it would be unwise to ignore that front altogether—in case the girl is right."

"We can't continue to argue the point," King Owen conceded. "Time is running out. If your wish is to defend the western hills, I shall lead a small party there. We can easily turn the enemy back before they clear the passage, with no more effort than standing on the cliff above and hurling spears and arrows at them. The bulk of the troops should be with you on the eastern front. I still think that is how the Norsemen will come, and a greater force with an experienced commander will be needed to fend them off."

Maeve struggled to keep her thoughts from showing on her face. Of course King Owen would lead the troops who would defend the western hills. That way he could let the Norsemen pass unimpeded so they could double back and ambush King Redmond.

"I shall take the girl and the Druid boy with me," King Owen continued, catching Maeve by surprise. "If what the girl says is true, being near the point of invasion may evoke in her a vision of what is to come." Though he sounded sincere, Maeve knew he wasn't expecting her to have a vision any more than he expected her to fly. He wanted her and Declan with him so he could conveniently arrange their deaths. He paused before adding, "But if it proves she has been lying, my men will keep the two from escaping."

"Better to divide and conquer," King Redmond murmured thoughtfully. "I am confident the girl has spoken the truth, but I would be a fool not to take precautions. I doubt either she or the lad would leave without the other. Therefore I shall bring the boy with me." He took the parchments from King Owen and began striding for the door. "Let us make haste."

Before the young people could be separated, Maeve whispered urgently into Declan's ear. "King Owen and Queen Ailsa are traitors. King Owen will allow the Norsemen safe passage through the gap. Then they will ambush the king and kill him."

Declan's eyes widened. "Are you certain?"

Maeve nodded. "I saw it in the king's dream."

"Then you'll be in danger!" he said, concern knotting his brow. "You can't go with King Owen!"

"I have to," Maeve argued. "I have no choice. But you needn't worry. It will be all right. I won't be harmed. I had a vision."

163

Declan hesitated. "Truly?"

"Truly," Maeve lied. She needed Declan to go with the king, and if he thought her safety was in jeopardy, she knew he wouldn't leave her. "You must convince King Redmond to give you a horse to ride south and hurry the troops still travelling. He'll expect you to direct them to him, but instead, you must bring them to the western hills to fight the Norsemen as they come through the gap."

She would have said more, but right then the two were swept into the hall. As Maeve watched Declan disappear around a corner, she prayed it wouldn't be the last time she saw him.

It amazed Maeve how quickly the soldiers fell into ranks and began the march toward the western hills, standards hoisted on poles at the front of each company to identify the clans. They were a ragtag lot—career soldiers with their swords and shields, maces and lances, tromping along-side farmers and tinkers with no protection but their leather jerkins, and nothing but staves and hammers for weapons. Some had no weapons at all. Most of the men were on foot, but those barking orders were on horseback. Of course King Owen led the way, and to Maeve's dismay, it was with him she was made to ride.

It felt strange sitting so close to the man who would see her dead, her back against his chest, the heat of his body warming her own, his scent twined with the air she breathed. To someone who didn't know King Owen's intent, he must have seemed chivalrous indeed, taking personal care of the seer himself.

He was a traitor but he had yet to show his hand, so Maeve played along. It made the situation more tolerable, and there would be time enough for the truth. Thankfully, he didn't try to engage her in conversation. When he did speak, it was to the captains flanking him.

Even with torches to light the way, Maeve found it impossible to see into the darkness, so—as always happened when she was left to her own devices—she allowed her mind to wander.

She thought of all the farmers and townsmen who'd dropped everything at home to serve their kings. Some were too old, others too young, and most were unprepared for a fight but willing to try. Maeve's father was one of those men. Somewhere in the throngs marching north to serve King Redmond was her father. And not for the first time. He'd fought for his clan and king many times before, but never against an enemy as formidable as the Norsemen.

It occurred to Maeve that Deirdre's husband, Fergus, would also be among those taking up arms for the king. His first time. Likely not his last though, unless—Maeve shuddered. She felt King Owen pull back to look at her, so she clutched her mantle tighter, that he might think she was shivering with the cold.

An image of her sister flashed inside her head—Deirdre in her dream, looking down into her baby's cradle, beaming and then tearful. And suddenly Maeve understood. Deirdre hadn't known if her child was a boy or a girl because the child was not yet born. She was looking into the cradle, imagining the baby, which led her to thoughts of her husband—gone to war. Knowing he could be killed, her joy became grief.

And now Maeve felt it as well. She hurt for her sister and wished she could save her from the sadness that had sunk its teeth into her. At the same time, Maeve was relieved. Deirdre wasn't the ice woman she seemed. She loved her unborn child—and her husband too. And she wanted to stay connected with Maeve. She had asked her to be there when her child was born.

Maeve sat up straighter so that she was no longer pressed against King Owen's chest. It was up to her to stop the Norsemen and keep Deirdre's family safe.

Chapter 21

The niche had been carved out of the clifftop by centuries of wind and rain. Maeve huddled within it and stared out at the night until her eyes burned. The moon, a feeble sliver of white, clung to the black sky, illuminating nothing. Shadows shifted before Maeve's eyes, and she held her breath, waiting for them to change into blood-thirsty Norsemen.

She glanced to her right. A few steps away, a guard stood as motionless as if he were cut from the stones themselves. Maeve knew that if she made the slightest move to leave this place, he would be on her in an instant.

King Owen's officers were on the clifftop too, talking and laughing in small groups—hardly what Maeve expected of soldiers preparing for a battle. But they weren't preparing for battle. It was all a sham for her benefit. She looked past them to the base of the craggy hills where the troops had settled in to wait, the blackness around them softened by small fires. Beyond that, out in the night somewhere was Declan, hopefully rallying the armies from the south to join the fight. She turned her gaze northward again and prayed the Norsemen would be slow. There was no telling how much time Declan would need.

The previous day's sunshine had melted most of the snow—all that remained were isolated patches—but it was still cold, and Maeve burrowed into her mantle for warmth. King Owen's army had left the castle in the early evening, but it had taken many hours to reach this place. She knew morning couldn't be far away.

She wasn't tired though she should be. It had been a day and a night since she'd last closed her eyes. But she was too anxious to sleep. Besides, if things worked out in King Owen's favour, she would soon be sleeping for eternity.

Where *was* King Owen? Maeve hadn't seen him since he'd left her on the clifftop some time ago. She studied the torchlit faces of the officers nearby, but his wasn't among them.

She went back to watching for the Norsemen. It seemed to her the sky was brightening. Morning was definitely getting nearer, which meant the Norsemen were as well.

"You watch as if you truly believe they will come."

Startled, Maeve spun toward the voice. It was King Owen. Where he'd come from, she had no idea, but she didn't like that he had sneaked up on her. Nor did she like the smirk on his face.

"They *will* come," she said coldly. "You know it as well as I do."

His smile vanished, and his eyes narrowed with suspicion. "How could I possibly know such a thing?"

"Because you arranged it," Maeve replied bluntly. There was no point playing cat and mouse any longer. The time for games was over. This might be her last chance to confront the man with his treachery.

For many seconds the silence hung heavy between them. And then King Owen laughed—a sound so unexpected it caught even the morning by surprise. "Ah, I see. You take me for the apple tree that quit the king's orchard," he chuckled.

"And the queen is the butterfly that left with you," Maeve replied, steadily holding his gaze. "Traitors, both of you."

King Owen's expression sobered, and his grey eyes turned to ice. "Hold your tongue, my girl—or lose it. You are speaking treason."

Maeve knew she should be afraid, but she wasn't. Unless Declan arrived soon with help, King Owen would kill her, regardless of what she said. "I speak the truth. You are a traitor."

He laughed again, but it was an ugly sound. "You saw this in the king's dream?"

"You know I did."

"Yet you failed to tell him. How odd."

"Not really. He trusts you. He loves the queen. He would not take kindly to the suggestion that either of you were betraying him."

Maeve must have hit a nerve, for King Owen scrabbled across the distance separating them and growled into her face. "It is he who betrayed us! We are simply taking back that which is ours."

The sharp rock behind Maeve dug into her as she tried to pull back from King Owen. "What are you talking about?"

"The kingdom! Don't pretend you don't know." His voice was hushed, but he was so close and so vexed that spittle came along with his words.

Out of reflex, Maeve pushed him away. To her surprise, he didn't resist. She frowned. "Are you saying the north country is rightfully yours?"

"This whole land is mine!" Maeve could tell it took a great effort for him to keep his voice down.

"How is that possible?"

"You don't know?" He seemed incredulous. But then he laughed scornfully. "No, of course you don't. You are but a child. You know nothing."

The hair on the back of Maeve's neck stood on end, and a retort sprang from her lips before she could bite it back. "I know that King Redmond's dream plainly foretold your treachery."

King Owen's arm snaked out and cuffed her so hard she cracked her head on the rock behind her. A bolt of pain shot through her skull, and tears sprang to her eyes. She blinked them back.

He laughed. "If you are hoping to win my favour, you are going about it badly. Would you like to try again?"

Maeve wanted to close her eyes until the pain pulsing through her head stopped, but King Owen might think her weak, so she bit the inside of her lip and looked him straight in the eye. She had to reason with him—but on his terms. "My whole life, Redmond has ruled the land," she said unemotionally. "And his father ruled before that. You were never the Great King."

"But I *should have* been!" he snarled, his cold grey eyes piercing her green ones. "I *should be* now! My grandfather was the *rightful* king of this land. Redmond's grandfather stole his crown."

"Ah," Maeve nodded. "Another war."

"Not a war!" King Owen sputtered angrily. "It was unlawful rebellion! Unspeakable treachery!"

War. Rebellion. Different words for the same thing. The crown had changed hands so many times, no one could say who the rightful king was. Still, Maeve needed to know King Owen's story.

At the risk of angering him further, she said, "My whole life, the kingdoms of this land have been at war. The rulers change more often than the weather. What makes your family's loss of the crown different from that of others?"

Once again, King Owen moved close to Maeve's face and growled out his story through gritted teeth. "My grandfather was Niall the Champion, so named for his prowess in battle. He and Redmond's grandfather, Seamus, were lifelong friends—as close as brothers until Seamus showed his true colours. My grandfather confided in him, and Seamus used that knowledge to steal the crown. He betrayed my grandfather and turned his own people against him!"

King Owen pulled back, and the sneer left his face. Maeve could see the anger draining from him. After several seconds he even smiled. When he resumed speaking, his voice was calm and even. He was the charming king once more. The change was so swift, Maeve didn't know what to think. Never had she seen anyone change moods so quickly. Truth be told, this incarnation of King Owen frightened her even more than his rage had.

"But now it's time to right the wrong," he said. "It has taken Ailsa and me much time to arrange matters, but today the crown will finally be where it belongs—on my head. Once Redmond—and those who follow him—are dead, his grieving widow will declare me king."

Maeve couldn't see the difference between what King Owen was planning and what King Redmond's grandfather was supposed to have done. But to say so would only anger King Owen again, and Maeve's head was still pounding from his last fit of temper.

"Clever plan," she said, "but aren't you afraid the Norsemen will turn on you after they've dispatched King Redmond? They are barbarians after all. As I understand it, they thrive on bloodshed and plundering, and you are letting them into the kingdom unchecked."

King Owen beamed. "I invited them. Their invasion was my idea. In exchange for significant treasure, they will do away with Redmond and his supporters and then return across the northern sea from whence they came. We have an agreement."

Maeve nodded, though she had her reservations. The Norsemen weren't noted for keeping their word. Once they were past the hills, they would have numbers and the element of surprise. They could roll over the entire land unhindered. No one would be safe—not even King Owen.

"So now you will kill me," Maeve said as a matter of fact.

King Owen sighed. "That was the plan, yes. However, upon further thought, it occurs to me that you might prove more useful alive. You are a seer, after all. I admit I had my doubts when you arrived at the castle, but you saw the meaning in Redmond's dream perfectly. The old Druid couldn't have explained it better himself. Yes, I could definitely use a good seer.

"Of course, you would have to pledge your loyalty to me, but I assure you I am generous to those who serve me well. Mind you, it might be a challenge convincing Queen Ailsa. She is not overly fond of you."

"I've noticed," Maeve said. "What about Declan?" She wasn't considering King Owen's offer for a second, but she needed to keep him talking.

"The lad who accompanied you to the castle?"

"Yes."

"Well, if he doesn't get killed during the ambush of King Redmond, I see no harm in sparing him. As a rule, Druids aren't much of a threat.

"It is your choice. Live or die." He shrugged. "Seems straightforward to me." He chuckled and gestured northward.

Maeve turned to look. In the distance, through the brightening morning, she spied what seemed to be a massive swarm of black ants. A cold dread spread through her.

The Norsemen.

Even though she'd known they were coming, their arrival was difficult to fathom. She didn't want to believe it. Everything was unfolding as she had foreseen it in King Redmond's dream, and the prospect of what would happen next terrified her. She'd thought that if she got the Great King to change his defence strategy, the Norsemen could be stopped, but what if she was wrong? With only King Owen's men here, there was barely any defence of this route. What if Declan failed to bring reinforcements?

"They should reach the pass within the hour." King Owen cut into her thoughts. "Once they're through, it's an easy march to the eastern hills. Redmond doesn't suspect a thing. He will be dead before he knows it. A pity really. I would have enjoyed seeing him suffer.

"But in case he wonders why there is no sign of the invaders yet and begins thinking they really are attacking the western hills, we have provided a diversion. He will be kept busy until the Norsemen arrive at his back door." He looked over his shoulder.

Maeve followed his gaze. Far off, she saw something dark moving through the pale sky. A bird, she thought, but then quickly realized her error. No bird had such a wing span, nor such a tail. There was a flash of orange and Maeve swallowed hard. No bird breathed fire. But the black dragon did, and it was headed straight for King Redmond and his soldiers in the eastern pass.

CHAPTER 22

Maeve knew too well the destruction the black dragon was capable of. Declan's tale had painted a picture of torment and despair she would never forget. Misery—the dragon was aptly named—was an evil creature that revelled in chaos. And locked in the pass between the hills as they were, King Redmond and his troops were easy prey. The dragon might not even need the help of the Norsemen to finish them.

They would have no way to defend themselves. They couldn't get near enough to the beast to use their swords, and their arrows and spears were as useless as stalks of straw against its scaly armour. Misery could rain his killing fire on them at will, wiping out entire sections of the army with one breath. His tail was just as deadly. Maeve was glad she was too far away to hear the tortured screams she knew would come.

She turned her gaze north once more and was shocked to see how much ground the Norsemen had covered already. She could now discern the individual warriors, though they were still too far away for her to make out their faces. There was no organization in their ranks—only hundreds upon hundreds of warriors tramping with purpose toward the narrow gap in the hills. With the rising sun glinting off the hammered iron of their helmets, they looked fierce. Maces, swords and axes swung easily in their hands as though part of their arms. Maeve shuddered to imagine the weapons leaping to action in battle. If Misery didn't destroy King Redmond and his troops, the Norsemen surely would.

Fear took root in her. If Declan didn't arrive soon, they were doomed. She cast her gaze in the direction he should come, but her view was blocked by King Owen.

"Intimidating lot, aren't they?" He nodded toward the advancing Norsemen. "I almost feel sorry for Redmond."

Maeve didn't answer. She was too consumed with thoughts of the mayhem that was unfolding. There had to be a way to stop it. If there wasn't, why had she been shown the meaning of the king's dream?

She looked toward Misery again. The dragon was fast approaching the eastern gap.

Then something else caught Maeve's eye. It was moving quickly across the sky from the southeast on a collision course with the black dragon. She squinted, trying to make it out. As it got nearer, she saw it was red. She gasped. It was breathing fire. It was another dragon! Maeve's heart leaped in her chest.

It was Riasc Tiarna!

Shouting broke out among the troops below the cliff. They'd seen the red dragon too, and in seconds a concerned buzz filled the air. Even the officers atop the cliff were pointing and jabbering urgently. Seeking direction, they turned anxious eyes toward King Owen.

In the dim early morning light, Maeve could see the colour drain from his face. "I take it the red dragon is not part of the plan," she remarked sarcastically.

As his head snapped in her direction, she was suddenly afraid. There was a wild look in his eyes. Had she pushed him too far? She tensed, waiting for him to pounce—to break her neck, slit her throat or perhaps simply throw her off the cliff.

But he wasn't even looking at her. His gaze was focused beyond her, on the Norsemen bearing down on them from the north. In the excitement of the red dragon's appearance, Maeve had forgotten about them, but now she turned back to look.

They had stopped. The entire army. And to a man, they were staring at the two dragons in the sky.

Maeve held her breath, waiting for them to make sense of what they were seeing. The red dragon had not been part of their arrangement with King Owen. The black dragon was to keep King Redmond's troops busy until the Norsemen were through the gap and able to attack from the rear. But now the red dragon was challenging their champion.

The Norsemen looked from the circling dragons in the sky to King Owen and his officers atop the rocky hills. Maeve could almost see them struggling to understand. Then she knew they'd worked out an explanation that made sense to them.

She was fairly certain she knew what it was.

They thought they'd been tricked. King Owen didn't intend to let them through the gap unimpeded at all. He wasn't going to pay them the treasure he'd promised. His plan was to lure them into the narrow passageway and massacre them.

That *wasn't* King Owen's intention, but the truth didn't matter. The important thing was what the Norsemen believed. Without any discussion or even an order urging them to action, the horde of warriors turned away from the spectacle of dragons and began charging toward the cliffs at full speed, bellowing like crazed animals and waving their weapons menacingly. They were insane with rage, and they wouldn't be appeased until they had killed every living being in their path.

The Norsemen were close enough now that the ground shook beneath them, and their war cries sent shivers of terror up Maeve's spine. She could see their faces—crimson with bloodlust beneath swaths of black war paint. Never had she seen anything so terrible.

King Owen had to do something. He had to stop them. She whirled around to tell him so, but he wasn't there. While she'd been paralyzed with fear, he had sprung into action—as had his army.

Maeve was relieved. At least they were going to

put up a fight, and they did have the better position, though the Norsemen were gaining momentum with every step.

But it soon became clear that King Owen's troops weren't preparing to do battle. They were getting ready to run! They were retreating. She couldn't believe it. They were cowards—every one!

Maeve knew she should run too. She should hide. But she couldn't move. It was as if she were under a spell. She couldn't even look away. This was the end. They were all going to die.

Chapter 23

Maeve turned back toward the Norsemen. Already they were into the gap—but only two at a time. If King Owen's men stood their ground, they could pick them off before they reached the other end. The bodies would build up, and the passageway would be impassable. At the same time, soldiers atop the cliffs could use their arrows to keep the Norsemen from scaling the rock walls.

But they weren't doing any of that. They were running away. The foot soldiers were fleeing like hunted rabbits, while the officers bolted ahead on horseback.

Within her niche in the rock, Maeve made herself as small as possible. Not that it would do any good. It was only a matter of time until they came for her. With no weapon to protect herself, she was as good as dead already.

Once the Norsemen slew King Owen and his soldiers, they would move on to King Redmond's troops. Then they would begin their march through the land, murdering and plundering as they went, until there was no one and nothing left. She thought of Enda and Bradan unprotected in the tiny woodland. They would be struck down. Maeve's father too. And Deirdre's husband. Eventually Deirdre too—and her unborn child.

Probably even her mother, though she might prove harder to kill. And all the Druids—no matter that they didn't believe in war and wouldn't fight back.

And Declan.

Maeve's chest began to ache, and she turned her gaze south once more.

Many of the Norsemen were already through the pass, but—Maeve sat up straighter and stared harder. Something wasn't right. King Owen's men were no longer running from them. They weren't running at all. Had they decided to stay and fight?

She was confused. Some of the soldiers were facing the oncoming Norsemen. Others had their backs to their comrades and were looking south. Around them pranced the horses of King Owen and his officers. Why had they stopped?

And then she knew. As Maeve watched, soldiers emerged from the woods in the east, west and south, moving steadily northward—company after company of kings' men, their standards flying proudly. It was *their* raised spears and swords that had turned King Owen's army back.

Maeve's heart jumped into her throat, and she began searching the field for Declan.

It was an impossible task. She would never be able to pick him out. There were too many men. Maeve knew Declan was out there—he had to be. But where?

She stood up to gain a better view, shielding her eyes with her hand and peering hard into the morning. Again and again she scanned the field, but she couldn't make out one man from the next.

The battle was now truly underway. Though the Norsemen were still pushing through the narrow gap, a good number had already reached the other side and were surging into the fight, their war cries piercing the morning. Likewise, the armies of the kingdoms loyal to King Redmond were closing in, their shouts less frenzied but equally determined. And caught in the middle, surrounded on all sides, was King Owen's army.

Maeve covered her ears against the clang of swords, the panicked whinnies of the horses, the thump of clubs and spears on shields, the ceaseless shouting and the death screams. The field was already so littered with bodies, Maeve had to look away.

She turned toward the eastern sky where Riasc Tiarna and Misery were embroiled in their own war. The dragons danced in the air, lunging forward and then pulling back. Round and round they whirled, the black and red of their writhing bodies twisting together, their scales glinting in flashes of fire.

Maeve frowned. There was something disturbingly familiar about this battle between the dragons. It was as if she knew what was going to happen—as if she'd seen it before. It was very like the dragon fight Declan had described in his tale by the Druid fire, but it wasn't that. Maeve was certain. She thought harder and then it came to her. *Of course!* This was the vision that had struck her like a bolt of lightning the day she'd picked mushrooms with Enda.

She held her breath. *Please let Riasc Tiarna be victorious.* For her, Riasc Tiarna was the key. If he could defeat the black dragon, there was hope.

"Maeve!"

Someone had called her name. She spun toward the sound. Her gaze zigzagged over the field, but she couldn't see anyone trying to catch her attention. As if things weren't crazy enough, now she was hearing things.

"Maeve!"

It sounded like Declan. Her heart began to race and again she scanned the battlefield. Where was he?

"Maeve!" And then a head popped up over the cliffside directly ahead of her.

"Declan!" she cried. She would have hurried to him, but the gap defining the passage below divided the cliff in two, and they were on opposite sides of the rift.

"How did you find me?" she cried once he had gained his feet and was as close as he could get to her without falling into the gap.

He had to yell to make himself heard. "I could see you. You were the only one up here. So I picked my way around the outside of the troops and climbed the cliff."

Maeve was relieved. She and Declan were still separated by the split in the rock walls, but at

184

least she could see him and knew he was safe. She grinned. "You found the troops."

Declan glanced over his shoulder at the ongoing battle. "For all the good it will do. The Norsemen are through."

Maeve looked to the north. "Not all of them. Not even half. We still have numbers. If our troops push them back, they can plug the gap and stop more from getting through."

"If that happens, they'll simply head for the other passage," Declan shouted, gesturing toward the eastern gateway where King Redmond and his troops stood in wait. "They're not going to go away without a fight."

She shifted her gaze to the dragons battling above the eastern passage. Misery made a killing lunge for Riasc Tiarna. Maeve caught her breath. It looked like Riasc Tiarna was done for, but at the last second he twisted sharply right, and the black dragon's mighty jaws snapped at air. The manoeuvre threw Misery off balance long enough for Riasc Tiarna to swing around and slash the black dragon's unprotected belly.

Even from this distance and over the tumult around her, Maeve heard the black dragon's shriek. The men on the battlefield must have heard it too, for there was a pause in the fight-ing—as if time had stopped. The wounded dragon rolled away from his opponent. His wings beat at the air, but they had no more effect than if Maeve had flapped her arms.

The great black body began to fall. Slowly at first, as though it might yet right itself and fly away, but then faster, spinning precariously and finally crashing to earth in a cloud of smoke and dust.

A cry from behind made Maeve jump, and she turned to see a Norseman's head even with the top of the cliff. But he had lost his grip, and as Maeve watched in horror, he toppled to his death.

"They're coming up the cliff!" Declan yelled.

Maeve didn't know what to do. She began backing away, but there was nowhere to go. After a few steps in any direction, the cliff ended. She was trapped.

Declan peered over the edge on his side of the gap. "There are more!" he cried. "Quick—find rocks to throw!"

Maeve searched the ground around her, but all she could find were small stones.

Look out!" Declan yelled. "Here comes another one."

Maeve looked to the cliff's edge to see the top of a Norseman's helmet. And then his hand was on the ledge. Not knowing what else to do, she rushed forward and stomped on it as hard as she could.

The Norseman howled but didn't let go. Now his other hand was on the ledge.

Afraid he would grab her foot, Maeve backed off, and as the Norseman's head came into full view, she shuddered. Wild red hair pushed out from beneath his helmet, fanning over his shoulders. His face was round and red and slick with sweat. A band of black kohl across his eyes and nose made him all the more terrifying. Maeve continued to back away. She looked over her shoulder. If she went much farther, she'd be over the south edge of the cliff.

A stone zinged off the Norseman's helmet, causing him to freeze. Shaking his head as if to clear it, he peered around, trying to see where the stone had come from. Spying Declan, he growled and resumed climbing.

Maeve screamed. She had never been more terrified in her life. She opened her mouth to scream again, but was stopped by a familiar voice in her head.

"Get as close to the south edge as you can and lie flat on the rock. Tell your friend to do the same."

Maeve pulled her gaze away from the Norseman and glanced skyward. Riasc Tiarna was winging toward them. But would he reach them in time?

"Back up and lie down!" she cried to Declan as she pointed at the dragon and threw herself on the clifftop. Declan quickly did as she said.

The Norseman saw Riasc Tiarna too, but he was too drunk with bloodlust to take heed. His eyes were on Maeve and he reached into his belt for his axe. As he started to swing it in a circle above his head, his face split into a maniacal grin, revealing teeth sharpened to a point.

Maeve squeezed her eyes shut. She didn't want to see her death.

"Cover your head," Riasc Tiarna said inside her mind. *"Things may get warm."*

She barely had time to do as he said before a torrent of blistering fire shot past her. Maeve opened her eyes in time to see the Norseman fly into the air and disappear over the edge of the cliff. He didn't even have a chance to scream.

Maeve looked up. As Riasc Tiarna passed overhead, he let loose another blast of fire that, judging from the cries that followed, took out the other Norsemen climbing the rock wall.

Then Riasc Tiarna was in her head once more. *"I am coming again. Prepare to climb onto my back."*

Maeve's stomach flipped, but she took a deep breath. *"We'll be ready."*

———

Maeve clung to Riasc Tiarna's neck with one hand, and Declan's hand with the other as her toes found a foothold in the dragon's scales. She'd been afraid of hurting him, but he'd assured her he barely felt her touch.

Declan squeezed her hand, and she smiled. The wind buffeted her ears and forced her to squint. Talking was impossible.

Part of Maeve was overcome with relief to be free of the cliff and the attacking Norsemen, but another part of her was in disbelief. She peered down at the world below. She was flying. *Flying!* She was on a dragon's back and she was flying!

It was like nothing she had ever imagined. She should probably be terrified, but she was too busy trying to take everything in.

"*Hang on tight*," Riasc Tiarna told her. "*I'm going to turn.*"

Maeve dug her toes into his scales as he banked and glided over the battlefield. It looked so different from the sky. It was just as awful—men were being struck down as she watched—but she saw that King Owen's army was finished. The reinforcements from the east, west and south had the Norsemen contained near the opening of the passage, making it hard for warriors to get through. That was why they'd climbed the cliff, she decided, noting that they were doing so again. Riasc Tiarna let loose a blast of fire, once more clearing the cliff walls.

As they continued eastward, she saw that King Redmond's army was north of the hills and marching west to confront the Norsemen still not through the gap. Soon the invaders from across the sea would be surrounded.

It looked to Maeve like the situation was under control. The invaders would be wise to retreat to their ships while they still could.

Finally, Riasc Tiarna glided past Misery. Once a formidable force, the dragon was now a lifeless black mountain destined to feed the land.

"*Our work here is done.*" Riasc Tiarna broke into her thoughts. "*It is time to get you back to the Druid.*"

CHAPTER 24

Maeve was excited. Peering around Riasc Tiarna's neck, she could see the small woodland where she and Declan had left Bradan and Enda. From the air it was a jumble of colours and textures — and much smaller than it appeared from the ground. As she watched, Enda came out from the trees into the clearing, shielding her eyes as she looked up. It was soon clear that a dragon diving out of the sky was not what she had expected — nor wanted. She began hopping around like a frightened chicken, scurrying this way and that and waving her arms until the shock of it became too much and she swooned to the ground.

By the time Riasc Tiarna touched down and the young people had slid from his back, Bradan was beside Enda, fanning her face and patting her hand. Maeve was pleased to see Bradan up and about. But Enda, as she regained consciousness, was definitely not happy. When she saw Maeve and Declan, she lit into them for scaring her half to death, all the while keeping a watchful eye on Riasc Tiarna.

Once Enda had done scolding everyone, there was much hugging and laughing and crying until finally it was time for Maeve and Declan to tell their story.

"King Redmond agreed with Maeve's explanation of his dream," Declan began when it was his turn to regale them with his version of events. "Bradan, your necklace was all the proof he needed to ensure his faith in Maeve. Apparently he had suspected for some time that King Owen's loyalty might be in question. Though I don't think he knew Queen Ailsa was involved."

"Perhaps he suspected but didn't want to believe," Bradan said quietly.

"Perhaps." Declan shrugged and continued. "At any rate, the second I asked to set out after the lagging troops from the other kingdoms, he said that was exactly what was called for. Regardless of where the Norsemen were coming from, he said, reinforcements were needed. He provided me with a horse and sent ten mounted soldiers to assist me. He even gave me a personal token so that there would be no problem convincing the armies that I was acting on his orders. We spread ourselves in a long thin line and began moving south. We didn't have to go far before we came across the first armies moving north. It was a small matter to redirect them. My only concern was that we wouldn't arrive in time."

"You nearly didn't," Maeve said. "I have to confess I was worried. If you hadn't climbed the cliff and slowed that Norseman down with the rock—" She stopped mid-sentence and shuddered. "I don't even want to think about what might have happened."

Declan eyed Maeve suspiciously. "At the castle you said you'd had a vision. You assured me everything was going to be fine."

Maeve grimaced. "I might have exaggerated." Then her face cleared and she shrugged. "But everything was fine, wasn't it?"

Declan shook his head and sighed. "That was a foolish thing to do, Maeve. You could have been killed." Then he nodded to Riasc Tiarna. "We both would have been done for were it not for Riasc Tiarna. He swooped in and with one fiery breath cleared the cliff of Norsemen. Then he carried us off on his back to safety. Thank you, Riasc Tiarna. We owe you our lives."

Maeve looked toward the red dragon and smiled. He was a magnificent creature. When she'd first met him in the cave, she'd known he was gigantic, but she would have died of fright if she'd actually seen him. Now he was curled comfortably on the ground, his head resting on his front legs, his yellow eyes half-closed, his long, spiked tail sweeping lazily through the grass. The morning sun glinted off his brilliant red scales.

"Yes, Riasc Tiarna," Maeve thought to him, *"Thank you. Thank you for everything."*

During the storytelling—in an effort to appease Enda, who was clearly uncomfortable in his company—Riasc Tiarna kept his distance. But when the tale was done he moved closer and bowed to Bradan, who acknowledged him with a solemn nod.

A lengthy silence followed. Enda tugged on Maeve's sleeve. "What's happening? Why are they staring at each other?"

"They're talking," Maeve whispered back.

"I don't hear any talking," Enda retorted. "I didn't even know dragons *could* talk."

"Not talking like you and I are," Maeve tried to explain. "It's more like they're thinking to each other."

Enda pulled back. "Thinking to each other? Get away with you! I never did hear of such a thing."

Maeve had been as surprised as Enda the first time Riasc Tiarna had spoken to her through her thoughts. She still didn't completely understand how that was possible. She only knew that it was. At least it was if Riasc Tiarna chose it to be. If he wasn't in the mood to carry on a conversation, there was nothing Maeve could do to reach him.

As she watched the Druid and the dragon exchange thoughts, she couldn't help wondering if it was the same with Bradan. Did he have to wait for Riasc Tiarna to initiate a conversation, or could he reach the dragon's mind when it suited him? Could he put up a wall in his mind to block thoughts from reaching him if he wished? Were these skills that could be learned? Could all seers and dragons converse through their thoughts, or was it something only Maeve, Bradan and Riasc Tiarna shared?

Maeve shook her head and sighed. So many mysteries. Would she ever find the answers?

After a moment, Enda tugged on Maeve's sleeve again and whispered, "Can you think-talk with the dragon too?"

Maeve bobbed her head. "Mmm-hmm."

"So what are they sayin' then?"

"It's a private conversation," Maeve told her. "Between only the two of them. I can't hear it."

Though she didn't say so, Maeve was also wondering what they were discussing. King Owen's betrayal and the battle with the Norsemen like as not. But they would be exchanging views and information only they were privy to. Maeve might not be able to hear their conversation, but she still had eyes, and she could tell there was a bond between the Druid and the dragon.

"*You have done well, young Maeve,*" Riasc Tiarna told her as he prepared to take his leave. "*You embraced your destiny and performed an important service for your king and the people of this land.*"

"*Will our paths cross again?*" Maeve asked, reluctant to let him go. She was going to miss him.

"*I am not the one to ask,*" he chuckled. "*You are the seer.*"

Maeve and her friends stayed at the woodland camp for another full day before beginning the journey to the southern region where Bradan,

Enda and Declan all lived. The weather had become quite balmy, and by the afternoon of the second day of travel, Maeve was so warm she slipped off her mantle. She shook her head to think that less than a week earlier they had all nearly frozen to death.

Walking beside Bradan, who was seated on the donkey, she thought about what lay ahead. She was both excited and nervous. On the one hand, this was an opportunity to explore new and wonderful things. No more was she a blacksmith's daughter whose days consisted of chores and constant scoldings. In her old life, her only respite had been an occasional afternoon selling eggs in the village. It was hard even to imagine that time anymore.

Even so, the prospect of being in a strange place with people she didn't know was unnerving. Though Maeve had already been living among the Druids for several months, she'd been close to where she'd grown up, near people she'd known her whole life. Now everything would be unfamiliar—the village, the people, the customs. She didn't know if she would fit in. She might be a misfit all over again.

Thankfully she had Bradan and Enda to help her adjust—and, of course, Declan.

"Wherever you are, it is not here," Bradan said, jarring Maeve from her thoughts. "But judging from the smile on your face, it was a pleasant diversion."

Maeve felt heat rush to her cheeks. "Sorry," she mumbled self-consciously. "I was imagining what it will be like where we're going."

"It is a comfortable place," he replied. "The village is somewhat bigger and busier than the one where you sold your eggs, but the folk are friendly. The Ruin is on the edge of the nearby wood."

Maeve regarded Bradan curiously. "The Ruin?"

He smiled. "It is the name of the place we live. Though its name would indicate otherwise, I think you'll find the accommodation more luxurious than our summer camp."

"Where will I stay?" Maeve asked.

"For now, with Enda and her mother," Bradan replied. "In time we can work out something more permanent."

Maeve nodded and tugged on the donkey's rein to urge him away from the grass and back onto the dirt track. She clucked her tongue. "Come on, Traveller," she scolded him. "It's not suppertime yet."

Swaying rhythmically atop the animal, Bradan chuckled. "Is that the beast's name?"

Maeve shrugged. "I don't know that he has a name. But I can't call him Donkey. He's become part of our family. And I think Traveller suits him, considering how much of it he's done lately." She lovingly stroked the animal's nose. "I shall be sorry when Master Finn returns him to his owner."

"We are beholden to Master Finn's friend.

Without the donkey, I don't know how I would have managed the journey."

Maeve wagged a finger at him. "You almost didn't! I knew it was going to be too much for you. You should have listened to me."

Bradan heaved a weary sigh and shook his head. "You are not going to let me forget this."

Maeve pretended to glare at him, but she soon gave up and laughed. "I was very worried about you. I'm just grateful you're finally on the mend, though Enda tells me you weren't a very cooperative patient."

Bradan sighed again and muttered, "That's another one that could do with learning how to leave a person be."

They walked on in silence. Maeve watched Enda and Declan up ahead, deep in conversation, though she didn't bother to wonder what they were saying. She was too caught up in her own thoughts. She turned to Bradan again and said, "Is Riasc Tiarna the dragon you met long ago?"

"He is," Bradan answered.

"I thought so," Maeve said. "He's also the dragon from the tale Declan told around the fire. Do all dragons live to be very old?"

"I can't say. But it seems likely—unless they meet an early demise."

"Speaking of demise, what will happen to King Owen and Queen Ailsa? Will they be executed?"

"Again, I don't know. It is within King Redmond's authority to demand their deaths, but I'm not sure he will. Even though their betrayal cut him deeply, he is not a vengeful man. And he loved Queen Ailsa. He may simply lock them away in a dungeon for the rest of their lives."

Maeve tried to imagine that. Endless days of iron bars, stone walls, stale water, wormy bread and no one but rats for company. Never to walk through the forest or feel the sun on one's face ever again. She shuddered. That would be worse than death.

Declan turned back and waved. "I think this is a good place to stop for the night. There is protection from the elements and plenty of firewood." He grinned. "This time tomorrow we shall be home."

———

After Bradan and Enda had bedded down for the night, Maeve and Declan lingered at the fire. For the longest time they sat staring into the flames without talking. They had no need of words. Being alone together was enough, and they were reluctant to break the spell.

Declan sighed and squeezed Maeve's hand.

She smiled and squeezed back. "You're anxious to get home," she said.

He took a deep cleansing breath. "I am. Seeing my family at the winter solstice reminded me how much I miss them. But it's more than that. I can't wait to show you my world, share my favourite places with you—where I go to think, to dream."

He chuckled. "Even sometimes to sulk. I am excited for you to hear the laughter in the brook that runs to the sea and work out the words in the wind as it whispers to the trees. I want to share spring with you there—watch the seeds sprout, the wildflowers bloom and the newborn deer wobble on untried legs."

Maeve's heart was so full she was sure it was going to burst. Never had anyone made her feel so special. Suddenly she wasn't the least bit afraid of what lay ahead. "I want those things too," she said shyly. "I want to continue to learn the ways of the Druids, and I want to learn all Bradan can teach me. I think I'm finally beginning to understand who I am—and why I am. I don't know what life I was living before, but this is the life I was meant for. I am so lucky."

"It is a good life, isn't it?" Declan murmured. "And in the late spring when we return to our summer camp, you can be with your sister when she has her baby."

Maeve nodded. "Yes. I am looking forward to that as well. It will give Deirdre and me another chance to get to know each other."

For a moment they stared into the fire, basking in its warmth and listening to the snap and hiss of the burning wood.

"You have important work ahead though," Maeve said.

"What's that?" Declan studied her curiously.

"Are you not a bard?" she teased.

199

"I'm working at it," he replied cautiously. "Why?"

"Because you have a tale of betrayal and war to shape and tell. That is no small undertaking, though I'm certain you are up to the task. After all, you were part of it."

Declan dropped his gaze self-consciously. "Actually I've already begun weaving the story," he said. "Would you like to hear?"

"Oh yes, Declan. Please. That would be wonderful."

He cleared his throat, took her hand in both of his and began. "In the days of the Great King, Redmond, there lived a young girl—a black-smith's daughter—who sometimes sold eggs in the local village. No one gave her much notice. She was but a simple lass who frittered the hours daydreaming. Or so folk thought."

THE END

AUTHOR'S NOTE:

The title for this book arrived in my head before the story did. That happens sometimes, and the funny thing is those are often my best books. So where did *The Druid and the Dragon* come from?

Druids have always fascinated me. I'm talking about the ancient Druids like the ones in this story. Modern Druids are quite different. They are completely open about who they are and what they do, but the early Druids were much more mysterious. That is probably why historians can't agree on what they were truly like.

But the Druids are only half the story. There is also the dragon. Though most people think there were no such creatures, dragons are included in folklore from countries all around the world. So what better subjects could there be for a fantasy than a Druid and a dragon? I could make them be and do whatever I wanted.

The story I decided to tell takes place in Ireland around AD 1000, though I don't say so in the story. That's because I didn't stay completely true to the geography and history of the area—I included enough factual information to make the setting recognizable, but when I needed particular details in the story, I took liberties. For instance, at the time this story takes place there were no oak trees or mistletoe in Ireland, but both those plants play a huge part in Druid folklore, so I included them. Also, money probably wasn't being used there at the time, but I included it in the story anyway. That's the great part of writing fiction—you can tweak the facts.

I had so much fun writing *The Druid and the Dragon*. I had a basic idea about what was going to happen, but as I wrote each scene, new and better ideas kept coming. It was almost like the story was writing itself and I was simply tapping out the words on the computer. Sometimes I would include bits for no other reason than to make the story more interesting. Little did I know those bits would reappear later and end up being quite important. Things like that make writing a lot of fun but also a bit eerie. It's like I'm not the writer at all—just the first one to read the story!

Though I spent a lot of time alone in front of my computer while the story took shape, I also relied on other people to help make the story the best it could be. The first ones to read *The Druid and the Dragon* (the first chapters anyway) were the ladies of River Writers, the critique group I belong to. Many thanks to my critique partners, Shari Green, Diana Stevan, Jocelyn Reekie, Sheena Gnos, Janet Smith and Liezl Sullivan. As avid readers and writers themselves, they helped me mould the story into shape so I could submit it to a publisher.

That brings me to my wonderful publisher and editor, Melanie Jeffs. We have worked together many times, but never before have we tackled a project of this genre and magnitude. Melanie helped me discover the *why* of the story and the characters' motivations behind their actions. She also helped me develop the backstory—plus all that other stuff editors do.

Then Jack Whyte, a renowned historical fiction writer, came along. He agreed to read the novel and share his thoughts on pertinent historical content the story still needed. It was a lot of work revising the novel over and over, but so worth it! With every rewrite I could see the story becoming richer and fuller.

The really telling part for me, though, was when my daughter, who always reads early drafts of my work, asked if she could let Elle, her daughter, read the first draft. Of course, I agreed, and in just a couple of days my granddaughter had completed the story. She loved it, which was encouraging, since she fell into the age range for the book's targeted audience.

But when she was giving me her feedback, she said something that struck a chord. "Grandberry, how can Maeve be a seer when she isn't a Druid?"

ABOUT THE AUTHOR

Many writers are or have been teachers. Kristin Butcher is not quite sure why that is, but she is no exception. Kristin taught for twenty years–everything from primary science to high school English. She hadn't planned to be a teacher; it was something that happened while she wasn't looking. She hadn't planned to be a writer either. Writing is just something she's always done. She's been doing it professionally now for nearly twenty-five years, and she still loves it.